UNDER HIS WATCH

LEONA WHITE

Copyright © 2024 by Leona White

All rights reserved.

No part of this book may be reproduced in any form or by any electronic or mechanical means, including information storage and retrieval systems, without written permission from the author, except for the use of brief quotations in a book review.

❦ Created with Vellum

ALSO BY LEONA WHITE

Mafia Bosses Series

The Irish Arrangement || The Last Vendetta

The Constella Family

Under His Protection

BLURB

Attacked. Saved. Falling...

For the deadliest man in the city.

One night. One alley. One hell of a plot twist.

I was supposed to marry a creepy lawyer.

(Thanks, Mom and Dad. Really.)

Instead, I'm claimed by a tattooed Adonis with a body count.

Romeo Constella. 30. Mafia royalty.

He saved me from a fate worse than death.

Now he's offering protection.

In his world of Gucci and gunshots.

His touch? Electric.

His kiss? Addictive.

His promise? Absolute.

"No one will ever hurt you again, bella."

But as rival families circle like sharks...

I realize I'm not the only one with a target on my back.

With every heated glance, every stolen caress,

The line between protector and lover vanishes.

Until one truth remains:

This isn't just about survival anymore.

It's about a love that could burn down empires.

Or get us both killed.

Under His Watch: Where danger meets desire and age gaps sizzle. Buckle up, buttercup – this steamy mafia romance is going to be a wild ride.

1

ROMEO

I strode through the main foyer of the guest house, grimacing at how much more work needed to be done. Wallpaper had to be removed. All this nasty old carpet had to go, and then the sanding and polishing of the old hardwood floors would follow. Updating appliances.

Franco set down another box of debris to haul out. Dust rose up, and we both sneezed.

"You're sure you want to deal with this place?" he asked.

He was more than the high-ranking capo in my family's organization. Franco Constella was a distant cousin, too, but at times like this, he resembled the brother I never had.

Never say never. I bit my tongue and refrained from groaning. In seven months, I might very well have a brother.

"Yeah, I'm sure," I lied.

I wanted something to keep me busy, busier than I already was as my father's right-hand man in the Constella Family. I was his second-in-command, and I handled a variety of responsibilities in that position.

"This old property needed work, and I want to put my blood, sweat, and tears into fixing it up."

"Oh." Franco nodded, looking around the house that was part of the extensive Constella real estate portfolio. "Sure. So you can, what? Purge out the guilt you shouldn't have?"

I shot him a hard look. I wasn't in the mood for him to tell me to get over the guilt. I was the only survivor in a fight three months ago. The lone man who lived. Three of our fine soldiers hadn't made it in a fight that Mario, a rat in the family, set up.

They shouldn't have died, not like that. And I would never "get over" it. That would be a dishonor to their memory.

He knew he'd crossed a line, being that harsh about this topic. Holding up his hands in a truce, he sighed and shook his head. "Hey, you know what? I don't blame you for wanting to move out of the main house while Dante and Nina are acting like lovebirds."

I chuckled, wiping the sweat from my brow. Fall was coming soon, but right now, the humidity of the late summer was sticking. We'd been moving junk and debris toward the door for hours. It seemed Franco wanted the empty-mindedness of manual labor too.

"I'm not coming here to renovate this place only to get away from them," I argued.

He scoffed. "You're not?"

"All right." I shrugged. "Maybe that is a factor in it." But I wasn't hiding. I'd always resided in multiple places. My "home" was the guest house behind the mansion my father, Dante, now shared with his fiancée, Nina. My cousin Eva lived in another such guest house. Franco, too. We all had our rooms and quarters in the big mansion, and we always would.

My father understood that I liked to diversify with my time and residence. I wasn't married. I wasn't shackled to anything but my job in the family, so why not have multiple options?

"But this place does need some attention." I gestured at the derelict surroundings, evidence of decades of wear and tear and even more of them with grave neglect. The house was something in the family and nothing we'd want to sell. My father never bothered with it except to discipline the new recruits, soldiers who came here one night and got a little too drunk and broke some old shit.

"That doesn't mean *you* need to be the one acting like some handyman contractor."

I shrugged. He wouldn't talk me out of it. "I wanted a project." I needed something to help me ignore how happy my father looked with Nina. I was glad for them both. He deserved love and loyalty after my mother died over thirty years ago. But this creeping sensation of jealousy was not something I wanted to endure any longer. I was sure it would fade. My father and Nina got together so quickly, and everything happened so fast between them that I hadn't really had any time to get used to my father no longer being only a workaholic and always accessible.

Eventually, it would be the new norm. My father would be a husband to someone again, and a father to their baby soon, my potential half-brother.

I was confident that a little space from them would help me get used to it. And maybe with that separation and not seeing them so wildly in love, this envy would loosen its grip on me.

"Hell, I wouldn't mind a project myself," Franco quipped, nudging his foot at a pile of busted wood in a heap from furniture that hadn't lasted the test of time. "I know they're not trying to rub it in our faces, being so all over each other all the time…"

I watched him, feeling like I'd recently grimaced just like he was doing now. "But it makes you realize what you don't have," I finished for him.

He smirked. "Yeah. Exactly."

Franco wasn't much better than me in terms of meeting and holding on to a woman for more than one night. He slept around here and there, but he was more focused on his work for the family than his own sex life. We were all like that. We had to be when so many lives were on our shoulders.

Years ago, Franco was serious about someone, but she was a distant memory now. I couldn't even remember her name if anyone were to ask.

"Don't tell me that we're going to suffer now that he's found his woman," Franco joked. "Like a contagion."

I rolled my eyes. "What, that we're all going to want to settle down since my father has?"

He furrowed his brow. "Nah, it won't happen. Not to me. I thought about it so long ago that it feels like another lifetime has passed." Catching a broom as he slid along the wall, he shook his head. "Besides, this isn't an ideal time to settle down. Or start projects."

I stuck my hands in my pockets. "Until something happens with this war my father declared on the Giovannis and the Devil's Brothers, *I* want something to busy myself with." It felt like an epic waiting game, watching our rival Mafia men and those bikers who'd recently come onto the scene.

He huffed. "Eh. You just need to get laid or something. Not start a fucking renovation."

"This is a project," I reminded him. "Something to fill my downtime. I'm not changing careers."

"And I'm not suggesting you are."

I wanted to groan. He was like a damn sibling, a brother. We always bickered like this. "Then what the fuck are you suggesting?"

He ran his hand through his hair. "I don't know. I've inhaled so much dust and shit in here helping you that my brain is fucked."

I laughed, walking toward the back to appreciate the fresher air breezing in through the open window.

"I'm suggesting," he said, following me, "that you get laid."

"Like that's a solution." It wouldn't be. Finding an easy piece of ass might have entertained me for a few hours, but that was it. Afterward, I'd be right back to my usual brooding self.

"I'm not saying it's a solution, but hell, maybe finding a woman to fuck could remind you that being a bachelor isn't always that bad."

I smirked at him, not buying it.

"Well, maybe getting laid would help you get your head out of your ass."

I stared out the window, watching the sun set further. All my life, I'd been a serious sort of person. A brooder. An introvert. A watcher and daydreamer, more comfortable in my own head than with others. Being "moody" wasn't just a phase I went through as a teenager. I wasn't emo or gothic in my adolescent years for the hell of it. I was a Mafia prince, born and raised with the laws of violence and corruption reigning supreme. No one was sane and lighthearted with an upbringing like I had.

Lately, though, my guilt about not preventing those three soldiers from dying had dragged me even lower. It wasn't depression, but deep-seated regret. It wasn't some sort of manic pit or any other psychological nonsense. It was hating that I couldn't have saved those good men.

"Romeo." He sighed. "You have got to stop beating yourself up for not being able to control those men dying. For not being able to control everything."

That was my most consistent flaw. I was a control freak, and that extended to the bedroom. Crossing my arms, I leaned against the window frame and stared at him. "Which is why giving me advice to 'just go get laid' is a joke."

He rolled his eyes, setting his hands on the open window frame. I didn't miss the slight flinch as he locked the muscles in his left arm. He was shot trying to defend Nina and Eva at a spa the night the MC men kidnapped Nina, and the muscles that the bullet pierced were still healing.

"I'm a hard lover," I reminded him. We didn't talk about this shit. We didn't deal with chitchats about women, sex, or marital goals. It was common knowledge, though, that I wasn't the ordinary man who could get off with just any easy pussy available. Franco knew. Back when we were younger and stupider, he accompanied me to the sex clubs where I acquired, then fine-tuned, my preference for the kinkier side of fucking.

"I'm sure there's got to be a seasoned whore around here somewhere who could handle you."

I raised my brows at him.

"For a price," he added hastily.

Buying sex no longer appealed. After witnessing the miracle of how much my father had changed since meeting his other half and falling so swiftly and seriously in love, it seemed like a cop-out to want anything else.

Who am I kidding? I'm not in any position to go looking for someone. Someone who likely doesn't exist. I'd need a patient and equally hard lover, and I wasn't sure she was real.

Besides, it was dumb to try to start something with anyone when I needed to start caring about myself more. Regardless of how often I was told to get over my guilt and move on, I struggled. If and when I could open up to letting a woman in my life, I had to do so knowing I was the best version of myself as possible.

I didn't love myself anymore. Not after failing my Mafia brothers.

In my darkest—and usually drunkest—moments, I got hooked on the idea that being loved again would make me feel whole. That finding a real match in a woman would help me accept that I was worthy of love. I wouldn't achieve that with some random hooker. Not even a skilled escort. It wasn't only sex that would make me change, but a *real* connection. A bonding experience of decent companionship. That was what I needed.

"Seriously," Franco said. "You're the Mafia prince of the Constella Family. Many women would be willing to entertain you. They'd volunteer to be your 'project' and keep you busy."

I deadpanned at him. "What women? The ones like Vanessa Giovanni?"

He winced at the mention of the woman who'd pursued my father so relentlessly since the beginning of the year. While seeing my father and Nina so sickeningly in love was an adjustment, I was very glad that I wouldn't have to put up with telling Stefan Giovanni's clingy daughter to get lost.

"Yeah, it's a bunch of stupid nonsense." He sighed as he stood and backed up, stretching his spine and arms. "We don't need a woman."

I shrugged. It'd be nice, though.

"We need to stay on guard. Keep our eyes open." He glanced at me, somber and serious. "With Dante focusing on Nina and the arrival of their baby, he won't be one hundred percent focused on the war with Stefan and Reaper."

I cringed at the mention of the Devil's Brothers MC's leader. Reaper was as nasty as they came.

"Which means we—you and I—need to handle the due diligence for him."

I held out my hand for him to smack it in our custom shake. "And we will."

My loyalty to my father and my family would *always* take precedence over any projects I might take on and any daydreams I might create about a fantasy woman who'd accept and love me for the twisted, dark bastard I was.

2

TESSA

My supervisor thought he was just "doing his job", but it came across more like he wanted to hold me hostage. I deadpanned at him as he flirted with my coworker, another waitress at the sports bar I'd picked up as a second job. The Hound and Tea was still my first job, but to make ends meet—or, in other words, to hand over money to my lazy father who claimed he couldn't work—I recently started waitressing at the bar on the edge of town. Waitressing was a universal service, and I appreciated the ease of being able to land another part-time job.

But this supervisor's policy to keep me waiting until he checked my section and approved my end-of-the-shift tasks was bullshit. If he'd stop flirting with my coworker and just check off the crap on my list, I could've left a half hour ago.

But noooo. He's gotta take his sweet-ass time trying to get in her pants and waste the rest of my night.

I sat up, frowning at my phone. It no longer was night. Nearing one thirty in the morning, it was way too late to be stuck here, waiting for permission to leave. He made me clock out already. I wasn't waiting and getting paid for my time, but I wasn't okayed to go.

As if I summoned the device to buzz, my phone rang before I could stick it back into my pocket. Spotting my father's name on the caller ID didn't make me smile. I grimaced. Then I considered letting it go to voicemail. When it did, I sighed in relief. Speaking with my parents was always a trying endeavor, and I preferred to avoid them as much as I could. With the many hours I worked, it wasn't too hard. They slept in, and I went to work. Rinse and repeat.

He called again, and I growled as I answered. "Hello?"

"Where the hell are you?"

I pulled my lips in, bottling in a scream of frustration. He knew damn well where I was. Where I always was. I had no life—social or otherwise. I was stuck in this hamster-wheel race of life, always slaving away for crappy pay and never getting ahead. "I haven't gotten off work yet."

Spying my supervisor leaning in toward the smiling waitress, I sighed and wondered if I should just leave and excuse my disobedience of not waiting for his dismissal for wanting to give them privacy.

"I need the car. You know this."

I rolled my eyes, then zoned out at the dark ceiling. They'd painted it black to make the bar look dimmer, but it looked tacky with chips and marks showing the white drywall underneath.

"You're getting really spoiled, you know that?" he snarled.

I laughed, choking on the irony of what he claimed. "Me? *Spoiled?*"

"Yes. You're a spoiled brat, expecting to just go where you please whenever you want, using *my* car."

"Oh." Anger rose up swiftly. "You mean your car that I use to go to work, both the jobs I hold down to give *you* my money? Because you're"—I cleared my throat—"fucking lazy, claiming you're too disabled to hold down a job?"

"Don't talk to me like that."

I shook my head, not feeling guilty in the slightest. "You sprained the joint of your pinky. Your pinky finger! Ten years ago!" It was the lamest excuse for disability ever, and his so-called handicap status was a goddamn lie because he was fully capable of playing his video games, drinking and smoking, and doing everything anyone with ten working fingers could manage as a fully functioning adult. He'd only realized that I could work for him, and that was the start of his stay-at-home, do-nothing existence.

"I need the car back so Joey and I can go to the fishing and hunting store tomorrow, right when they open, so we get the door buster deals."

"I'm sure I'll be home before then."

"Did you get good tips tonight?"

I scowled, fisting my free hand and wishing I could reach through the call and punch him. How could he call himself a parent, only caring about me for the purpose of taking my money?

"I don't understand why you ever put up with those jobs." His raspy chuckle, dry from all the years of smoking, grated on my nerves.

It was a no-win situation. I worked and worked and worked, knowing he'd demand a steep cut of my income because he and my mom were so generous as to let me live with them. And I worked and worked and worked because I refused to consider the alternative that he was hinting at right now.

"If you just stopped and thought about it, you could've been married already. And none of us would have to work."

My patience and goodwill snapped. "You *don't* work!"

"And you wouldn't have to either if you just married Elliot already."

I shook my head and closed my eyes. I'd oppose that scenario until my dying breath.

"It's your own fault you have to work all these long hours," he taunted.

No, it wasn't. He was at fault for the shitty life I had. He insisted that I pay him a steep "rent" to let me live with them. If I could make money and keep it, I'd move out. I'd strike out on my own.

The only way he'd let me out of that agreement was if I moved out—after marrying Elliot.

Hell no. Over my dead body will I ever give that guy hope.

Elliot Hines was a creep. A pervert. An ugly man with, I was now convinced, an even uglier soul. My parents were old friends with his parents, and in some weird, twisted connection as long-standing acquaintances, they'd all gotten it into their heads that I should marry Elliot.

They'd concocted the pairing when we were young. He was hideous and cruel then, the mean bully of a kid no one wanted to be friends with. He never dated because no women wanted to put up with him. But my parents would never quit pressuring *me* to become his wife.

"He's loaded, Tessa," my dad reminded me unnecessarily. "He's making millions, and you can't get over yourself long enough to realize how easy life could be if you just married him."

Easy? Selling myself, selling my soul, would be easy?

"No. I've told you and Mom a thousand times that I don't want to marry him, and I'll tell you a thousand times more. I am not marrying Elliot."

"Why not?" he demanded.

"I don't like him." That should've been the simplest reason to adhere to. Why should I be pressured to marry someone I had no connection with?

"Tough shit. You think I 'liked' your mother when we met?"

Covering my face with my hand, I rubbed and held in a groan. *I don't want to hear this.*

"She was a nagging, whiny bitch. But hey, she gave decent head and—"

"Stop." I cringed. "Stop talking."

"Not *liking* Elliot is a stupid excuse. You don't have to like him. Just marry him so we can get easy money. Roll over and let him have his way, put up with it, and get over it."

Staring at the floor, I wondered what happened to him to make him such a terrible parent, such an awful man and an intolerable human. This was ridiculous.

"What's not to like about him, anyway? He's more successful than anyone you'd ever meet on your own," he scolded.

"Money isn't everything," I argued. "Just because he's a lawyer and makes a ton of money doesn't mean he's actually successful." The last time I talked about Elliot with my best friend, Nina, we read over the recent news about Elliot's win in court. He seemed corrupt, likely a bad seed in the legal system. *But then again, the legal system is crooked anyway, right?*

"Money isn't everything?" He cracked up, laughing so hard I couldn't hear the late-night talk show in the background on his end of the call. "Oh, sure. Money isn't everything according to the spoiled young woman who knows nothing about life. If it's not everything, Little Miss Independent, why are you still living at home with me and your mom?"

"Because ever since you realized I can make money, since I got my first job when I was sixteen, you demanded that I give most of it to you." He was a world-class asshole and an expert at using guilt to force me to pony up. No teenager should ever have to pay for a household, but he'd insisted upon it.

"You don't like my rules, then move out," he snarled.

I wanted to, so badly. Nina and I used to dream big and talk about leaving our shitty lives. She was stuck living with her good-for-nothing brother, Ricky. I was stuck at home with my parents. But during the slow moments of waitressing together at the Hound and Tea, we talked about saving up to move in together, to be roommates and really be conservative with our money to splurge on a vacation someday.

I hadn't heard from her for a month now, though, and I missed her terribly. I couldn't fault her for pretending to date Dante Constella, the wealthy crime lord she'd run into the night Ricky lost her in a bet to the notorious motorcycle gang.

Based on her last call, when she admitted that things were *really* getting heated up between her and Dante, I assumed all was well. Her phone no longer worked, though, and I wasn't sure whether she'd changed her number or not. Maybe living the easy life as the kept woman of a rich man had her wanting to shed her old identity completely.

No. That can't be it. Nina and I were best friends. She'd reach out sooner or later. This call with my dad was souring my mood so much that I was thinking negatively.

Nina would contact me. I counted on it. Until she did, though, I would continue to wish that she could rub a little of her luck on me. It would be a miracle if I could meet a man I'd actually be attracted to. A normal, good, and decent man who'd encourage me to get close and maybe lose my virginity.

The pause in my dad's rambling rant jarred me. I'd tuned him out, thinking about Nina and missing her fiercely. Now that he'd stopped to catch his breath, I realized it was dumb to sit here and let him shout into the void.

"I'll have the car back before you go to the fishing store with Joey," I said, dull and deadpan, before I hung up.

Never mind his caring whether I got sleep. Never mind his concern about his twenty-two-year-old daughter getting home and relaxing after her long double shift of work. He was selfish to the core, and I knew better than to think highly of him.

Finally! I shot up from the stool I was waiting on while my supervisor watched my coworker. She strode toward the bathroom, winking at him over her shoulder. This was my chance. I tapped his back and cleared my throat. "Hey, can I go home now?"

He frowned at me. "Jeez. Being patient wouldn't kill ya, you know?"

My anger boiled hotter. *Fuck you.* I smiled, forcing this polite expression, and pointed at the checklist he still held. "Sorry to interrupt." *Not.* "But I'm expected at home."

Rolling his eyes, he went through the list. Everything was done. Of course, it was. I might hate my jobs, but I did them well, trained for too long to be a perfectionist and people pleaser. The more perfectly I behaved, the more likely I wouldn't annoy men—that was the unspoken lesson my parents taught me.

I exhaled in relief as I strode out of the bar.

Walking through this area of the city at almost two in the morning wasn't a bright idea. I liked to think I had a decent amount of street smarts, but I wasn't aware of my surroundings.

My feet ached, and my back was sore. In my mind, I calculated the tips I'd gotten today and I figured out how much I could try to keep and hide from my dad. Stuck in my head, I made the biggest mistake of all.

I didn't notice the group of three men following me toward my car until it was too late. A sixth sense of feeling like I was being watched prompted me to look back, glancing over my shoulder.

They made eye contact, smiling with a predatory glee. Then as one, they ran after me.

"No!" I screamed it, terrified as I tried to sprint to my car. In my haste, I tripped and fell. Coins scattered from my apron as I dropped. Dollar bills sprayed out over the pavement.

Before I could register the burn and pain from tripping and falling, their hands were on me. Dragged off and silenced with a dirty hand over my mouth, I panicked.

Forget hating my life and feeling like I had no way out of it.

I had to suffer an even worse fate now.

3

ROMEO

Even though I spent all day working at the house, hauling out bags and bundles of ripped-out wallpaper, I wasn't calling it a night yet.

Just like Franco and I decided, we would keep up with gathering intel for this war my father declared against the Giovanni Family and the Devil's Brothers MC. So, by day, I avoided being idle by renovating that house. And by night, I met up with the spies I'd delegated to follow the bikers.

"I'm sorry I don't have anything new to tell you," Andy, one of my spies, said. He shrugged as he cradled a beer bottle between his hands. He was a bourbon drinker, but to blend in near this part of the city and stay undercover, he was trying to look more like a middle-class, blue-collar working man.

I sighed and shook my head. "No. It's all right." I sat up straighter, regretting that I might have pulled my back dragging debris and junk out of the house earlier. I was only thirty-one. I wasn't old yet. But maybe I was overdoing it.

He chuckled, noticing my wince. "Work out too hard or something?" He smirked before taking a sip of his beer. "Like father, like son."

I grunted a laugh. My father did enjoy working out a lot. He was so much of a gym junkie that he renovated and arranged for a state-of-the-art gym at the mansion. However, it seemed Nina also enjoyed exercising. I stopped going to work out there as often when I walked in on them getting a quickie in between reps.

I furrowed my brow, annoyed that I couldn't shed this envy. I wanted that. I wished for that feeling of just fitting with someone so perfectly, but I doubted any such woman was made for me like that.

"I hope no news is good news," Andy added. He'd been undercover spying on the Devil's Brothers bikers for over a month now. Several others were always watching them. Together, they didn't have much to report.

The Devil's Brothers MC was new on the scene here. Motorcycle gangs came and went. Mafia families, like the Constellas, Giovannis, and even the Domino Family, were organizations that had been established many generations ago. The Dominos were taken out by the bikers, but that wasn't the norm. Still, there was much to learn about these elusive bikers trying to claim a place of power.

"I wouldn't say that no news is good news," I replied seriously. I saw no point in lying. "Because they know that we've identified them as our enemies."

Andy nodded, frowning at his beer bottle. "I hope Nina is recovering from being kidnapped."

"Oh, she's doing fine. Happy about the baby and in love with my father." I shrugged.

He grinned, looking the part of an ordinary man teasing a friend at this bar. "It's pretty wild. Once they marry, she'll be your stepmom."

I gave him a deadpanned look, not wanting to humor him.

"She's what, like a couple years younger than you?"

I exhaled long and hard, not taking the bait.

"All right. All right." He set his empty bottle on the bar. "Enough teasing. It's not like there aren't other couples in the Family with years separating them."

My father and Nina had a significant age gap, but if it worked for them, who was Andy—or anyone else—to judge?

Maybe that's what I need. A younger woman to teach and educate about how hard I like it. An experienced, older woman would likely be too damn independent to consider being submissive.

"Anyway," Andy said, bringing me back to the reason I came way out here to chat at the bar. While it was disappointing that he didn't have much intel to share about the movements of the Devil's Brothers men, I was glad to have a chance to check in with him. Ever since I'd failed to save my other Mafia brothers, I'd adopted a habit of trying to supervise them all.

"I'll keep looking and listening."

I clapped him on his back. "Good. I appreciate it."

Andy huffed. "Well, it's my job."

True. And he'd do it well. "Just make sure you report to me."

"Not Dante." Andy raised his brows. "He's the one who put me on this assignment to begin with. I gotta admit, I was surprised when you showed up."

I nodded. "Yes. Me. I'm taking over this part of preparation. All intel about the MC will be reported to me."

"What about Franco?" he asked.

"He's heading up gathering the intel about the Giovannis." We'd schemed a two-pronged approach. With Stefan aligning with Reaper, combining the rival Mafia Family with the bikers, Franco and I could divide our attention in half. This spared my father from getting too involved.

"My father needs this time to focus on Nina. They're getting ready for the baby. And after that, planning their wedding." I stretched again, hating the tension in my muscles. I didn't intend to stay long. It was clear that I needed a good night of rest. "Franco and I intend to stay on top of getting the intel we need to attack those fuckers."

Andy didn't argue, nodding and standing. I stood as well, tossing several bills to the bar top to cover our drinks and then some.

"If you ask me, Dante's been overdue for some love in his life."

My father had been all work and no play for too long. "Agreed."

As we walked toward the exit of the bar, I noticed the few stragglers, likely regulars who would stay until last call. This place was a hole in the wall, a dump that no crime family, club, or gang considered their turf. As such, it was ideal for meeting up with spies. Andy and I agreed on another meeting a couple of weeks from now, and I watched as he turned to the east and headed out into the night. For the sake of not looking like we knew each other out here, where anyone could be watching, we parted without any further farewell.

Fatigue slithered through me as I walked toward the west, where I'd parked in a dark lot. I was exhausted, mentally and physically, but it was impossible to slack in checking my surroundings. I was alert as I strolled through the alley, always ready for an ambush or attack. That was simply part of the job description, I supposed.

This alley interested two long rows of businesses, but no skyscrapers blocked out the streetlamps. Dim lights offered me the way forward. Other than the distant thumping bass from nightclubs that would stay open for hours into the morning, it was quiet. Save for my footsteps, it was silent back here, giving the illusion of peace. The city never truly slept, though.

Nearing the lot where I'd parked my car, I heard something else, though. Grunts. Muffled noises from someone's mouth. When a whimper reached me as I walked past the rear entrance of another smaller bar, I sped up.

I knew those sounds. I'd caused those sounds. Grunts that paired with the force of flesh against flesh as I fucked a woman hard. Muted moans of someone being gagged. The whimpers could only be the result of someone in pain or afraid. That was what prompted me to sprint faster and intervene.

I'd tortured and killed many people in my line of work. It was almost hypocritical of me to want to intervene in someone else performing either of those tasks. The difference was that I knew my actions were always just—in the name of protecting my family and organization.

The three man holding down a woman and fucking her was not just. Not one goddamn bit.

I ran faster, oblivious to keeping guard. If they had another person looking out, I wouldn't know it.

As red colored my vision and my heart raced with the adrenaline rush of impending violence, I stared at the gang rape and anticipated the sweet promise of making them regret it.

"Hey. Hey!" The man fucking her ass noticed me first. His sick grin shifted into a scowl of confusion. Then he glared with anger. "Fuck off, man."

My fist landed on his face, cutting off his orders. I punched him so hard that he flew back, slamming to the pavement.

"Whoa. Dude—"

I kicked the other man from behind, preventing him from finishing his words. He'd been fucking her from the front, sandwiching the terrified blonde. With his legs splayed apart, his balls were exposed and vulnerable. I slammed my shoe between his legs, smashing him where he was most vulnerable in the middle of the act.

He was too slow to fall. I grabbed him as he cried out and doubled over, wrenching him off the woman.

Her big blue eyes widened at me. Behind the tears, she stared at me with horror.

If I weren't consumed with rage, I might have slowed down enough to realize she feared me as *another* man to rape her, but that wasn't the case. "I won't hurt you," I told her as I turned to the third man.

He was still in the process of pulling his pants up, clumsy with trying to stow his wet dick inside and zip up. It seemed he'd already had his turn.

"Fuck you. Just fuck off, dude. Nothing to see here," he said with a bravado that wouldn't hold up once I reached him.

Grabbing his hair, I slammed his head down to my knee. Once. Twice.

Crack.

There it was. With his nose smashed in, blood spurting out fast, I spun him. Still holding his hair, I cinched the strands tighter, damn near scalping him with the hold. "Nothing to see?" I punched him directly in both of his eyes. "Yeah. Nothing to see." I'd be shocked if he wasn't blind after that.

I let the man drop to his knees, glad that my back blocked the woman's view. She was sobbing, heaving for air past the fabric they'd tied around her mouth. Already violated and terrified, I didn't need her to witness my wrath.

Before the other two men could run away, staggering on their knees from my hits, I pulled out my phone and took pictures of them both. They escaped, fleeing quickly, but I wasn't done with them. I'd only begun to exact my vengeance.

After I helped this woman to safety, I'd find them and finish the lesson of what happened when they preyed on someone weaker.

"I won't hurt you," I repeated to the woman lying on the pavement. She shook, crying and scrambling to get away, and my heart ached at what she'd suffered.

I didn't know who she was. I didn't know where she came from. But she sure as hell hadn't deserved this.

I crouched lower to help her, keeping my hands up and letting her see that I wasn't trying to hurt her. My shoe slipped as I stepped on her ripped, bloody panties, and my rage intensified. She was wounded, by them or otherwise, and my instinct to help kicked in.

"Let me help you."

She sobbed harder, shaking her head as I reached out and pulled her skirt back down.

Her hands were bloodied and scraped. So were her knees. Blood streaked down her inner thighs, and that sight promised those men's deaths.

They'd taken her virginity in the worst fucking way possible.

"I will help you," I vowed.

I didn't know what convinced her. Maybe she'd simply given in, so scared that she couldn't fight back.

How? I struggled to concentrate after the rush of intervening and stopping those men.

Fuck. I didn't know what else to do with her so broken and bloody. If anyone else came close, they'd assume I'd done this. That I'd raped her. Calling the cops was out of the question. I was a Mafia prince, a wanted man. I didn't work with the law, but I had to help this woman.

"Let me help you." I reached out to scoop her into my arms, and I carried her to my car. She cried, sobbing and fighting to get free, but I held her close until I got her to my car.

Unsure of what to do with her, I figured I would drive her to my house. As I reached the door to the backseat, I hoped I could follow through with what I'd promised her—to help. I'd been wanting a project, but I hadn't considered something like this. Like her.

4

TESSA

I fell back against the seat as the man put me in the backseat. He hadn't broken a sweat, not in fighting those men nor in carrying me. Despite my furious wrestle to get free, he held me tight and didn't come close to dropping me once.

Now I had a better chance. The need to survive charged through me, and I funneled all that rabid energy into kicking at him. Both my feet flew to the side. My kick wasn't effective as he dodged to the side and avoided the impact.

I tried again, and again, using my whole body to lunge at him. The need to run, and run *hard*, wouldn't fade.

When those men ganged up on me, they overpowered me. It seemed that this man was determined to do the same. I'd locked my mind when those men used me so horribly. It was a dark, numb stasis that I snapped out of the second I heard this newcomer rush up close and beat them off.

Now, terrified all over again at the idea that this bastard would do worse by me, I was filled with that sharp need to fight. To flee.

"Calm down."

He did *not* just say that. He did not. I flung out harder, punching and kicking to no avail. On my back on the seat, I was overwhelmed with the panic that this guy was going to rape me as well. My stomach revolted. My heart banged wildly with a superspeed pulse that dizzied me. I couldn't catch my breath, and this asshole dared to repeat that inane command.

"Calm down."

This stupid fucker. Telling a woman who was just gang raped to *calm down*. I glared at him, letting him see the anger in my eyes at the lamest, most idiotic thing he could tell me.

Still, he caught me and kept me in the car. "Calm down." This time, he said it slower. His voice carried authority, but he wasn't shouting. He wasn't begging for me to chill. He wasn't mocking me. He was simply instructing me to deescalate the situation.

Heaving a hard breath through my nose, I stared at him and stopped fighting as much. Feeling his hands on me—anywhere—was too much. After being raped and violated like that, I couldn't stand the contact of anyone even near me. That was how strong the need was to run and scream. To cry and drop into a ball of sorrow and anger.

"Get in the car," he ordered.

Fuck no. Fuck this. I wasn't going anywhere with him. He'd beaten off those other men, but I didn't know what that meant. Was he trying to help himself to me, beating up the others just so he could cut in line to rape me? Did he plan to drive me away, hurt me more, then kill me?

In the back of my battered and stressed mind, already fucked from the trauma of what just happened, I knew that being transported wouldn't bode well. In kidnappings, that was the rule they preached at self-defense courses. Never be moved. Stay in one place to be found.

"Get in the car." He lowered his gaze to my knees as my lower legs hung off the back seat. I saw the indecision in his eyes. He was about to grab my legs and force me in the car, but he seemed to understand I'd lash out even worse if he touched me again.

"Now." He looked to the side, ever so slightly. This twist gave me a view of his profile, and it showed the same look of anger that facing him fully did.

"Now," he said again in a low growl. He rested his hand on the top of the car and leaned in without touching me.

The white fabric of his T-shirt stretched. All muscles. He was a brute, a bodybuilder of a tall man. Through the material of his shirt, his tattoos bore a sharp contrast, every line and shading making him look that much more dangerous, that much more of a rebellious bad boy.

He was strong. He could overpower me just the same as those others did. But he was calm, confident, and taking charge.

"Get in the car. I said I would help you."

How the fuck can I trust you? How the hell do I know what that means?

While I had the evidence of him scaring off those men and intervening, I had no clue who this guy was. I'd never seen him before, and I would've remembered a masculine face like his, hard angles, rugged features, faint beard, and all. His light blue eyes were strikingly bright, piercing me with the demand to look at him.

He clenched his teeth, tightening his jaw, and it emphasized the ink he had up along his neck. Every inch of him was hard, toned muscles, and I shrank back further from him. This man could kill me with a simple twist of his hands. Until I knew he meant what he said, that he'd help me, I couldn't get over the gut-wrenching anxiety at the thought of his easily killing me.

"Dammit," he growled, looking away as though the sight of me disgusted him. He was furious, but not *at* me. "Get in the car."

He seemed mad but in control of his anger. It wasn't a gentleness, but something similar.

I scooted back over the seat, feeling the smear of blood that would likely cover the cushion. He didn't care. He didn't flinch, waiting until my legs were further in the car.

I was insane to believe him. I would be crazy to *ever* trust another man on this planet after what happened to me in the alley. But I recognized that he would get his way. He knew it, too, waiting me out. I had no chance to get around him. I couldn't fight my way to freedom. Glaring at him and praying he'd drive me to the cops, I obeyed and kept scooting all the way back into the car.

"Hurry. Before the cops come." He shut the door as that warning rattled in my head.

No!

Before the cops came? I had to go *to* the cops. And he wanted to avoid them.

I was in a worse situation than before, but instead of crying or succumbing to the lure of blanking out and going numb, I resorted to more fury.

He slid into the driver's seat and immediately engaged the locks. They weren't standard issues. No matter how much I tugged on the handle, I couldn't open the door.

"Stop," he instructed, calm yet mad.

He pivoted in his seat, flashing a knife.

I screamed—muffled with this gag—and shrank away from his reach.

"Stay still."

How about fuck no! He wouldn't kill me easily. I wouldn't behave and just let him stab me.

"Stay still," he repeated as he reached back toward me. His fingers gripped my gag, not *me*, and he deftly sliced off the nasty rag.

I coughed, breathing too quickly. As I licked my lips and gasped in steadier inhales to better fuel me through this panic, he turned, started the car, and sped off.

Falling back from the force of his speed, I rubbed my face and worked on reclaiming a natural closure of my mouth, licking my lips, swallowing hard, and working my jaw. I sat there and processed that he'd removed the gag.

If he wants to kill me... Does this mean he's a sociopath who listens to his victims scream?

"I want to help you." His voice hadn't lost that hard edge, but again, a tiny voice had me thinking he wasn't mad *at* me.

"Where are you taking me?" I demanded, trying a few times to get the words out with my croaky voice.

He replied by handing me a sealed bottle of water from the cupholder. "Drink."

"Don't tell me what to do." In any other circumstance, I would've felt bad to talk with that snark. He was my rescuer—maybe—and he was due some respect for that save. But I wasn't myself. I wasn't thinking straight. I was locked too deep in survival mood to know if I could trust this man or whether he'd actually rescued me at all.

"Where are you taking me?" I said again before he could respond to my snark.

"My home."

"No." I shook my head, spilling some of the water that I'd drunk. His home? So he could keep me captive there? "No."

He narrowed his eyes at me through his reflection in the rearview mirror. "I'm taking you to my home to help you." As he said the words, he furrowed his brow, almost as though he questioned his decision.

"No. That's not..." I shivered as flashbacks of those men raping me filled my mind's eye. It'd just happened, and blocking out the memories wasn't something I'd perfected yet. Tears burned anew as the car went over a pothole, jolting me on the seat.

My ass hurt. My vagina felt so raw. Reminded of the horror I'd suffered, I slipped back into that scary state of wishing I wasn't alive to feel this anymore.

The shame. The fear. The anger. They coalesced into an angry storm that had me freaking out with the chance to voice it all.

"No one" —I choked on a hard sob— "No one will want me now. I'm damaged. I'm all damaged goods now." I couldn't see past the blur of tears, and I swore my soul was crushing my heart. My chest was too tight. My head was a heavy mess of darkness and despair as the first reactions punched through me.

"Elliot won't want me now." And in a truly sick way, I felt free. I was glad that I would finally have an excuse to not be with him. Never in a million years would I have wished this to happen this way. Never. But if I had to take hold of a silver lining...

"Who is Elliot?"

I shook my head, almost forgetting for a moment that someone else could hear me say such a thing. Something that didn't fucking matter among everything else. Elliot wasn't a priority. Surviving what happened to me was.

"Your husband?" he guessed as he drove.

No. Never. I sniffled, trying to breathe steadier.

"What are you talking about?"

"Nothing." This man was a stranger. I didn't know yet if he was a friend or foe. With his bravery to fight off my rapists, I wanted to believe he was a good person, a caring stranger who refused to be an innocent bystander.

Telling him anything about myself seemed like ammunition that I didn't want him to have.

"What's your name?" he asked.

I caught his hard glare in the mirror again, and I shook my head, refusing to answer.

"Who are you?" he tried instead.

"No one."

He cursed, so quietly that I couldn't hear. When he stopped at a light, he frowned at me. "Do you want me to take you to the hospital?"

He should. I needed medical help of some kind. Blood was leaking from me where it shouldn't. I was ripped. Bruised.

Raped. I was raped. Admitting that fact was too cruel of a fate to accept, and just thinking it brought more hot tears to my eyes.

"No hospital?" he guessed from my reaction.

I couldn't speak, drowning in this agony again. I needed to get checked out, but I couldn't afford any medical care. I was past due in paying off my dad's old debts, and my mom worked as an LPN at one of the nearest hospitals.

Facing her wasn't possible. I wasn't sure if I ever could after what those men did to me. Not because I felt disgusting, but because she'd realize I was damaged goods and wouldn't be an option for Elliot anymore.

"Do you want me to take you home?"

I shook my head. "No. I can't face my parents."

"You live with your parents?"

I began to nod but stopped short. He was prying for information again, and the more I stuck to closing my lips, the better. I didn't know if I could trust him. My trust was shattered too far.

I could not go to my parents. Not now, and I wondered if I ever could. I was supposed to be their good girl, the obedient daughter they wanted to marry off to a high and mighty lawyer.

"Then let me help you inside." He parked, and I just barely had time to register that he'd stopped at a huge but old house. It wasn't rundown to a point that it looked like a vacant dump, but I saw signs of it needing a lot of care.

Before I could protest or even think of anything else to say, he opened the back door and held his hand out. Walking would be a challenge with the soreness between my legs, but I was determined to avoid touching this man. This stranger. This… knight in shining armor?

I stood, eyeing him closely. Paying attention to him and this place was a distraction from the distress in my mind and heart. But I was too cautious to engage in anything more than putting a name to his face. Until I could think for more than a minute without resorting to tears and panic, I had to take this slowly.

"What's your name?" I asked as I stood and took a step from the car.

"Romeo." He closed the door, watching me as though he feared I'd fall. He'd asked me who I was and I had yet to answer. But he didn't pressure me to reply now as he gestured for me to walk up the steps. The first one I climbed on burned my knee, and I nearly crumpled to the ground.

"Let me help," he said as he pulled me into his arms and carried me up the steps. I didn't have time to freak out at his touch because the heavy pause after his words indicated that he was still waiting to know my name. He didn't cop a feel. He didn't glance down at me with any hint of the predatory evil that those three men had. In his blue eyes, I saw something that seemed a lot like concern.

This stranger caring about me… It was a wild thought that I yearned to hold on to.

I swallowed hard. "Tessa," I said quietly as he brought me inside. "My name is Tessa."

5

ROMEO

"The bathroom is right there," I said as I put Tessa down on a chair in what might be a living room one day. When I started fixing up my great-great uncle's house, I hadn't counted on needing to offer a woman in distress comfort. My first-aid supplies were lacking.

Her hands and knees were covered in blood. I saw the smears of red on her thigh too. She needed to be cleaned up, but I wasn't sure if she could stand or handle the task herself. Or if she would allow me to help her.

She flinched under my touch, and I didn't blame her. Not after what she faced. Forcing her to let me wipe off her wounds would probably do more harm than good, but I didn't know how else to get her to follow my instructions.

"I'll find a rag. To help clear the blood. But…" I stood back and ran my hand through my hair.

But I can't undo that this even happened. And I wanted to. Something about her made me turn into a beast wanting to avenge her. It wouldn't right this wrong, but I was tugged into the need to make her feel better.

She pressed her legs tighter together and lowered her gaze. Her chin dipped, but not so much that I couldn't see the tremble in her lower lip.

I hardened myself against the need to act. To move. To punish and kill. Battling the instant rage of finding her abused, I tried to control myself and at least look calm, even though I felt the opposite of it.

She was a stranger, but something indescribable and undeniable had me wanting to make her look at me without fear and shame.

"I can…"

I didn't finish. I strode away, worried that my anger and frustration would rise to a degree that I couldn't manage it. Heading toward the kitchen, I sought out the package of rags and wipes that I bought for tidying up this place. Before I grabbed the cleaning materials, I took out my phone and sent a message to Andy. He was a spy in the area, and I bet he'd have luck with this impromptu assignment.

Romeo: *Find these men and send me their location.* I attached the pictures I took of the two men before they ran off.

Andy: *On it.* He didn't ask a single thing. That was why he was such an excellent soldier to rely on.

I filled a bucket with warm water, and after I tucked the packages of wipes and rags under my arm, I carried everything out to Tessa.

She hadn't moved, still dipping her chin against her chest. I was glad she hadn't been reduced to crying again, but I imagined she would be hit with flashbacks and memories of what had occurred.

There was no way to dismiss it or sweep it under the rug, and I wasn't going to suggest that. The only answer that made sense to me was to kill those motherfuckers, and I would as soon as Andy or someone else in the family identified them. In the meantime, I could help Tessa clean up some of this blood.

I dragged a chair closer, facing her, and sat down before I wetted a rag. I began on her knee. She flinched, but I was counting on that reaction. She was still in a survival mindset, and I wouldn't hold that against her.

"Easy," I cautioned, reaching out to wipe the blood again.

She let me press the cloth to her, sitting so still with her gaze on my hand. Over and over, I cleared off the blood, finding the scrapes long and angry but not too deep. No wonder she struggled up the steps. The gash covered her whole joint and all the skin was inflamed.

I moved on to her other knee and repeated the slow and careful cleanse. Keeping my hands steady and not rushing so as to avoid startling her, I got all the blood and debris out of the wounds. Of at least *those* wounds.

"I tripped and fell," she said, numb and dull.

I nodded and cleared my throat. "I see that."

"They ran after me as I left work."

"You work near there?"

She nodded, sniffling a bit. "At the sports bar. I just got done working and… and they…"

I gently set my hand on her thigh. "I saw." Sparing her the need to talk again, I got up and dumped out the bloody water. With another bucket of clear water, I resumed cleaning her knees. Over and over, I replenished the water.

On one trip to the kitchen, I texted Danicia to come over. She was a former emergency room doctor we'd saved from the Domino Family, and she agreed to be on call, on the down-low. If Tessa would agree to any medical help, official or not, she would do best with a female.

After I did the best I could with cleaning her knees, I wrapped bandages over the injuries. Then I moved on to her hands and cleaned up the injuries and scrapes that ran up from the heels of her palms.

Holding her hands felt different from when I cleaned her knees, and I was overwhelmed with how much she pulled me to her. How much she called me closer and encouraged me to care.

Running up to intervene was instinct. I was a killer. I was a Mafia prince who preferred the darkness and somberness of life. But seeing an innocent woman like that triggered something in me at that moment.

"I'm…" She swallowed hard, raising her dark-blue gaze to mine. The vulnerability in her eyes cut through me, and I wanted to erase the pain she had to be feeling. "I'm still bleeding." Admitting that, so quietly and sheepishly, was clearly so hard, but I admired her tenacity and bravery to speak up.

I knew. I already knew she had to be bleeding and wounded between her legs. When she exited the car, I saw the smears on the cushions her short skirt couldn't hide.

I hung my head, exhaling heavily. Those men would be dead before the end of the night. I vowed it as I stared at the floor, but when I lifted my face to meet her eyes directly, I tried to soften my expression so she wouldn't misinterpret my anger as something she was responsible for.

"I called a doctor."

She reared back, tugging her hand out from my grip. "No. No doctor. No, I can't afford—"

"Not like that." I shook my head. "Not at the hospital. Danicia used to work at the emergency room, but since we helped her out of a…" *Shit.* I couldn't tell her that we saved Danicia when she was caught in the middle of a hostage situation. That would scare her more.

"Out of a what?" she asked, furrowing her brow.

"Out of a delicate situation," I improvised.

She narrowed her eyes and tilted her head to the side. "Who are you, Romeo?"

I sighed.

"You said you wanted to help me out of the alley before the cops came. Are you on the run from the cops?"

I stared at her, knowing that confessing I was a Mafia man might frighten her even more.

"Are you a secret agent?"

I didn't laugh *at* her, but the idea was so ludicrous that I couldn't hold in a chuckle. She frowned, almost pouting at me, and I shook my head. "No, Tessa. I'm not a federal agent."

"Then who are you? *What* are you that you would avoid the cops in an emergency like that?"

I licked my lips, hesitating. "I'm in the security industry, but in my line of work… I've learned that many cops and authorities we should trust are corrupt."

When she nodded, I raised my brows. "You agree with that?"

"Sort of." She shrugged one shoulder. "Yeah. I do. I've, um, heard some stories, and I wonder sometimes."

"Well, Danicia used to work with the cops when they'd bring victims like you in. She's able to bring a rape kit and help you get more comfortable."

I stood quickly, recognizing that she wanted distance from me after I said the word *rape*. "Danicia was an ER physician for twelve years before she came under my organization's protection."

She frowned again. "Like the witness protection program or something?"

"I guess that's a close enough comparison."

Danicia arrived, and just like I knew she would be, she was kind, take-charge, but compassionate. When she asked if she wanted me to stay during her "check-up" and Tessa said no, too embarrassed and on the verge of tears again, I led both women up to the master suite. I'd spent the most time making this room livable, and Tessa could have privacy here.

Once I knew she was safe and in good hands, I called Franco.

"Can you come watch over the house?" I asked. He was only a five-minute drive away.

"Yeah. But why?"

"I have someone here. And I need to go out and take care of a little business." That was code for a variety of things, and Franco knew better than to ask any questions.

While I cleaned Tessa's wounds and let Danicia in the house to look her over, Andy had surpassed my expectations. He'd found all three of the guys, because they stopped in the same hotel Andy had a room at. Maybe it was fate. Luck. Coincidence. I didn't care what happened to line up their paths, but Andy grabbed them all and brought them to the nearest warehouse we owned in the area.

He didn't need to be told what to do. That was the beauty of having well-trained and experienced soldiers.

Heading to the location he gave me, I let all the pent-up anger I'd tamped down rise to the surface. Rage coated my conscience. Dark energy had me tense and impatient to inflict pain.

I arrived primed and ready to kill those motherfuckers for ever daring to touch Tessa, to prey on her and make her cry.

"Need help?" Andy asked as I walked in and tugged on gloves. I wanted the men's blood on my hands, but in a rhetorical sense. If I got too messy killing them, I'd need to take even longer to clean up before I returned to Tessa and saw to her care.

I had no clue whether she belonged to anyone. She said she lived with her parents and was afraid about something with a man named Elliot.

But she would be there, and I wanted to be the man to comfort her and see to her recovery.

"No."

Andy nodded and backed up. Before I walked in, I did a double-take at the short dagger hanging on a hook. I grabbed it, and inside the room where the three rapists were tied up, I took my time carving out lethal lessons as to why they shouldn't have ever tried to hurt her.

I didn't hurry because I wanted to give Danicia and Tessa more than enough time and privacy, and also because I relished in the satisfaction of torturing these rapists until they begged for death. On that point alone, I was tempted to let them bleed on slowly and suffer.

Andy was still posted outside the room. He was a spy, but I knew he'd handle helping me out with this too.

"Dispose of them when they're dead."

Andy leaned to see past me as I tugged off the gloves. "Want me to kill them and get them out of here quicker?"

I glanced back at the bloody, messy room. "No. They've earned every second of agony."

"Yes, sir."

It felt good to kill the men who'd raped Tessa, but as I drove back to her in that shambles of a home, I realized that this was quickly becoming more than an ordinary night of being a Mafia prince and a ruthless killer on the streets.

Tessa deserved this act of revenge because she was an innocent, preyed upon and brutally violated.

But a sneaky alternative entered my mind.

I cared. A lot. I wanted to pay back those men personally, even though Andy or any other soldier could've handled it for me.

And it was because Tessa, whoever she was, was already getting under my skin in a way no other woman ever had.

6

TESSA

Danicia put me at ease. Her eyes were kind and her smile wasn't one of pity, but of sympathy.

"I know exactly how this feels," she said after Romeo introduced us.

I was glad he left the room, but I was nervous to see him go. Since he'd stopped those three men from continuing their attack and halted them from raping me any further, I considered him a source of security. With Danicia, though, I instinctively knew that I would be safe under her watchful care, and in a different way from what Romeo could offer.

He'd cleaned up my hands and knees from when I fell on the pavement, but I wanted the peace of mind of medical assistance for the rest of my injuries. "You do?" I asked her, shocked that this tall, fit Black woman could've ever been raped.

Romeo had to have told her about my situation when he was changing out the bloody water, but I wasn't offended. I wasn't worried that he'd spoken about me with a stranger. Not when she seemed so calm and confident.

"I was. Many times." She sighed as she sat on the edge of the bed, not touching me and giving me space.

I appreciated her respect for distance. Still, the topic that we spoke about cut through my soul.

I was raped. Each time I reminded myself of the cruel fate that my mind wanted to dismiss and ignore, an involuntary defense mechanism, I shivered and fought tears all over again.

"If not for Romeo and his people, I would've endured worse."

The long scar along her jawline suggested that she'd already suffered something gruesome. I supposed in a small way, I was fortunate that those three men hadn't tried to hurt me sadistically with a knife or gun.

"It just seems so…" Wrong. Horrible. Shameful. "Surreal," I said at last. "You always hear about statistics and know that this sort of thing is possible, but it seemed like a remote and faraway thing that wouldn't touch me."

She nodded. "I agree."

I didn't want to talk about it. She'd listen. I knew she would. Romeo said she was an ER doctor, not a shrink. But I wanted so badly to tamp down the thought of what happened to me. I wanted to smush it down and ignore it all for as long as I could.

"How did you meet Romeo?" I asked instead.

She didn't react to how swiftly I changed the subject.

"He was very critical in helping me get out of a challenging predicament."

Hmm. Another vague reply.

"Would you like me to examine you, Tessa? If you're concerned about—"

I laughed once, a hysterical bark of a sound. Then I sniffled and nodded. "I'm concerned about everything. But I'm…"

She pulled out a mini bottle of whiskey. "This might ease your nerves."

"Thank you." I seldom drank. Nina and I sometimes shared a beer or two after work, but I needed that numbing buzz. I opened the sealed bottle and took a quick drink, hoping the burn down my throat would quickly turn into a foggy mindset that would further dull my memories.

As Danicia examined me, carefully and telling me every step of the way what she was doing, I tried to block out the fear and stifle my tears. It was similar to a yearly check-up with the gynecologist, yet not.

"Do you want to tell me what happened?" she asked gently.

I didn't, but some obedient part of me recognized her as a doctor, as a figure of medical authority, and the dam broke. Like someone else was narrating my life, I told her in a monotone, unattached way how the three men had raped me, taking turns to put themselves in both of my holes.

"Only one entered me… there…" My pulse raced as she cleared up the blood near my anus.

"With his fingers or his penis?" she asked clinically.

"Both? I shut down and…"

"I understand. The tear is superficial," she said, "which will heal faster."

I didn't even want to think about how I'd heal. I felt so filthy inside out that I wasn't sure I ever would.

"They used condoms?" she asked.

I shrugged, losing my control on blocking it all out mentally.

"I see no evidence of semen," she explained. "And that's very good."

I choked on a weak laugh. "Good, huh?"

"I imagine they were cautious of STDs." She smirked. "Selfish motherfuckers. But that's a blessing for you. Less risk of anything passed to you." As she finished up, she sighed heavily. "I'll run some labs and make sure, anyway. Blood work, these swabs I collected. I'll cross every T and dot every i."

"Thank you."

"Do you have a family doctor you'd like this information to be shared with?" She took off her gloves as I sat up and lowered my legs beneath the sheet.

"No." I shook my head. "I don't want my parents to know." And with Mom working for the largest healthcare network in the city, she'd find out quickly. If not from insurance claims, then from snooping on my chart.

"I have my ways to circumvent the insurance forms and—"

"No. Please." As I relaxed in the bed, the exhaustion of the long day and night added to the warmth from the whisky. I yawned, but afterward, I raised my brows in surprise that I could be tired.

"Okay." Danicia nodded as she continued to explain how to care for my wounds, and she set out a few things from her bag that she brought with her. Antibiotics, salves, creams, painkillers, and another bottle of whiskey. She wasn't a conventional doctor, that was for sure, giving me alcohol should I want it.

I listened the best I could as she explained how to tend to my wounds, and with her mention of the house being guarded, I sank further under the illusion that I was safe here. Even if I wasn't, I was too weak to fight this fatigue.

After she backed out of the room and shut the door, I closed my eyes. Just for a moment. One minute turned into more, and I slept on and off for so long that I was disoriented when I woke. Sunlight streamed through the curtains, signaling that I'd slept in for a long time, a rarity I never had a chance to enjoy.

Waking up in an unfamiliar place was jarring, but once I spotted the lampshade that I'd zoned out looking at during Danicia's examination last night, I tried to slow my heart rate. My blood pressure would likely stay high for a long time, but I attempted to convince myself that I was safe here. I hadn't been moved. No one, it seemed, had come into this room and bothered me. I was still in the sleep shorts and panties Danicia had offered me. My clothes were intact.

That's a lot more than what I can say about last night.

All the memories rushed through me, and I counted my breaths with the square method to avoid being locked down in fear again.

It didn't work. The more I tried to resist panicking as I woke up more clear headed after a night of sleep, the deeper the horrors persisted. Getting over the trauma of what those men did to me would take more than a single night of sleep. I knew that. But I spiraled and freaked out.

In this room, I was grateful for my privacy, but I hated that I was alone at the same time. I couldn't go home to my parents. I couldn't even bear facing them at all, certain they'd judge and punish me for "letting" myself get raped.

A fleeting wish came of calling Nina. She was my best friend, and this was exactly what friends were supposed to be there for—talking down panic attacks. But she wasn't here. I hadn't been in contact with her. And I felt ashamed to even tell her about what happened.

Why? Why is this stupid sense of humiliation so strong? I hadn't done anything to get raped. I fought. I pushed back. But I was hit with such a hard dose of shame.

A knock sounded on the door, and it jolted me from staying in my mind.

"Tessa?"

I furrowed my brow at Romeo's voice, unsure how to face him, either. "Yes?"

"Can I come in?"

I winced. It was his house. He didn't owe me anything, not even my privacy after all he'd done. Stopping those men. Getting me to safety. Cleaning my cuts and getting me medical aid.

"Yeah." I wasn't sure I wanted to talk to him, but I felt even worse to be rude and shut him out.

My God. I'll be a people-pleasing, obedient girl until I die. I rolled my eyes.

"Did Danicia help?" he asked as he entered and sat in the chair next to the bed. He roved his gaze up and down me as I sat up in the bed, but it wasn't a creepy stare. More like something a concerned friend might do.

"Yes. She did. Thank you."

He nodded, seeming pleased about my reply. "She's on call should you need anything else." Glancing at the array of materials and medications she'd left on the nightstand, he added, "Even to help with the wounds and bandages."

I held up my hands, showing him the gauze. "Thanks. This should help a lot."

"I want to help," he said, gentle and sincere. "Please know that."

Why? Emotions clogged my throat, and I breathed through the sting of pending tears.

"What's wrong?" he asked, so observant to notice I was about to bawl again.

I never cried. Never. But this time, it wasn't the memories of my trauma that got me like this. It was him. That he cared. Following the solo attempt of talking myself down from dwelling on the flashbacks, his genuine concern was touching.

"No one does."

"What?"

"No one ever helps me." Nina used to. We helped each other the best we could, but we dealt with the same hand of cards and weren't in any position to really improve each other's lives.

"I will."

I wiped my cheek, hating the tear that slipped down. "Why? We're strangers. I'm—"

"You're a woman I want to help. And I will." He leaned forward, resting his elbows on his knees as he clasped his hands together. "I have, and I won't stop."

I stared at the angry gash on his knuckles. "Is that from punching that man last night?"

He nodded.

Sick anger built stronger within me, chasing out the despair a bit. "I wish you hit him harder."

He cocked his head to the side. "Do you mean that?"

I nodded.

"Then it's my pleasure to let you know he's dead. All three of them are."

I held my breath, letting his simply stated words filter through my mind a few times. I wanted justice, but that was fast. And grisly. "Dead?"

"Yes."

I opened and closed my mouth a couple of times, staring at him in a very new light. Strangers. We definitely were strangers, but I was plugging in more details about him.

He killed those men. He was a murderer.

Yet, I wasn't afraid. "You…?"

He nodded.

"Holy shit." I breathed it out in a rush, accepting his claim and letting it sink in.

I sat across from a killer. A murderer. A man who killed others was my rescuer. "Are you going to kill me?"

He snorted a laugh. "No."

I licked my lips, feeling a rush to ask so many things but intimidated to speak at all. I'd never met a killer before. I didn't associate with criminals.

But is he one? He wouldn't tell me who he worked for, and I had so much to learn. But not right now.

"Will you…" I cleared my throat to get the words out. "Are you going to keep me here against my will?"

"No." He shook his head. "I will do whatever you want me to do, Tessa."

I gaped at him, wondering if he was joking.

"Just ask," he prompted.

I sniffled, hit again with the need to break down.

No one, and I meant no one, had ever been that generous and considerate to me before.

"Can you…"

I heaved in a shaky breath.

"What, Tessa?" He furrowed his brow as he slid further to the edge of the chair.

"Can you just… hold me?" I asked, my heart cracking at how badly I needed that basic comfort.

Even from a deadly stranger like him.

7

ROMEO

Dammit.

I stood just close enough to reach her. Wrapping my arms around her felt natural, like she belonged in my embrace. I kept my hold loose, just in case she'd regret what she blurted out in that broken tone.

Last night, she flinched from my touch. Now, she clung to me. Her fingers twisted the front of my shirt, and with a heaving, desperate inhale that almost sounded like a sob, she pressed her face against me.

I gave in to the lean and gathered her in my arms. She probably wasn't aware of how she made space for me on the bed, but I pushed closer until I sat next to her.

"I've got you," I said, rubbing my hand over her back as she curled and slanted into me. This wasn't a hug. It was a full-body hold that she seemed to need.

I wasn't so serious and cold that I lacked physical touch. I wasn't impervious to the need for human contact. Over the years, I got that need met from dalliances with whores and one-night stands. When I was a young boy, my father was always ready to envelop me in a hug just as often as he was prepared to teach me about the hardness of the Mafia life.

How fucking long has it been since you had anyone?

I rubbed Tessa's back and let her cling to me as she steadied her breath. Hugging me seemed to help. She didn't suck in air like she was on the verge of hyperventilating or crying. As I held her and offered her wordless comfort, I replayed the sad admission she'd shared. *"No one ever helps me."*

I grew more and more irritated at the fact that this woman might not have anyone. No help. No support. No one and nothing? She didn't deserve that.

"I will help you," I repeated. I'd lost count of how many times I'd told her that. And I would echo it many more times, as much as I had to until she knew that she was no longer alone.

She snuggled closer, pressing her cheek against my chest, and I rested my chin on the top of her head. This was a simple, fundamental hug, but it opened the gates to my feeling so much more.

I'd only met her a day ago, not even. For hours, Tessa had been in my life, and already, she'd prompted me to go to such extremes for her. To fight for her. To save her. To avenge what was done. And now, to just be with her. Sitting and calming down from the high anxiety of the conversation we'd had so far.

Her warm, slender body fit so well against mine, and when I sighed several moments later, she did the same, breathing deeply and settling against me.

I told Franco that I wanted a project. That I needed something of a new purpose in my life to distract me from the guilt about the three soldiers dying. Tessa, whoever she was, seemed to be the missing piece I needed.

I was smitten without even knowing much about her, and I hoped that now might be the time to learn a thing or two. She hadn't recoiled from learning I killed those three men. Maybe it was a sign of her grittier conscience, that she wanted revenge and was happy—not appalled—that I'd taken their lives. Her acceptance of my being a killer was a huge first step to count on in connecting with her.

"Would I be a horrible person to want to say thank you?" she asked softly, tracing her finger back and forth on my shirt. It seemed like an abstract movement, not a deliberate caress, but it felt so good. "For... for removing them?"

"No. And you're welcome."

"Are you a hitman?"

Sometimes. "I'm a man who wants to take care of you," I reminded her, avoiding giving her more information about myself. Asking her questions about herself would probably turn into sounding like an interrogation, and I wanted to avoid that. Shifting her so she could lean on me but also face me, I rubbed her arm and gazed into her dark-blue eyes.

No glossiness of tears shone now, and I wanted to keep it that way. "Who are you, Tessa?"

She shrugged. "Just a waitress from that sports bar—" Her brows dipped and she scoffed. "Oh, God." When she lifted her hand to tuck her hair behind her ear but failed in keeping her blonde tresses back, I took over and did it for her.

I was already so damn smitten that I'd take any excuse to touch her. To comfort her. "What's wrong?"

"My car." She shook her head, using the action to nestle in against me. "Well, it's not mine. I could never save up for one. It's my dad's."

Your dad that you want to avoid going home to, I recalled. She'd been so adamant about not going home.

"He expected me to bring it home last night. Well, I guess this morning. He wanted to go somewhere." Her frown deepened. "He called me just before I was allowed to be done with my shift, actually. He'll be so damn mad that I didn't bring the car back."

"Is he always controlling like that?" I asked. I hoped that rubbing her arm would serve as a physical cue to relax even though I was pushing for answers. This moment felt a lot like aftercare, when I would make sure my lover could handle how hard I'd been during sex.

"Yes. Him and my mom both."

"Is that why you don't want to go home?" I asked.

"No. Yes." She blew out such a hard breath that the short, golden strands of her bob lifted from her face. "They have strict expectations for me."

"Including bringing a car home on time?" I almost said it mockingly. "Tessa, what happened to you is *not* your fault."

She swallowed and nodded. "I know. Logically, that makes sense, but I can't imagine telling them about it. They expected me to marry the son of their friends, and now that this happened…" She shrugged.

"Is that the Elliot you mentioned last night?"

"Yes. Jeez. What else did I blurt? I don't remember all that I said last night."

"Just that you were worried about someone named Elliot not wanting you anymore."

"Yeah. Because I'm damaged goods now."

I gripped her chin with enough force that she lost the sadness lurking in her eyes. She narrowed them, frowning up at me.

"You are not damaged goods."

"I'll agree to disagree on that."

Stubborn. But she wasn't annoying me. I liked that she had some grit.

"Who is Elliot?" I asked instead.

"Elliot Hines. My parents are old friends with his parents, and they got it into their heads that Elliot and I should get married. They thought of it when we were just kids, but now that I'm an adult, it seems like it's gone from being a silly comment and idea to an actual obligation."

"Hines?" I asked. Something nagged me about the guy's surname.

"Yeah." She studied me. "Why?"

"Sounds familiar."

"He's been in the news every now and then."

"Why?"

"He's a prominent lawyer in the city, for the J.R.G. law firm."

I nodded. "I've heard of them." When the Domino Family fought the Devil's Brothers, that legal firm was mentioned by the spies and soldiers gathering intel for us.

"My parents have been pushing me more and more to marry him. They think Elliot equals wealth, that if I marry him, *they* wouldn't have to worry about money again."

"But you don't want to?"

She shook her head, keeping her gorgeous, wide-open gaze on me. I knew she was telling the truth. I saw the sincerity in her eyes. "No. I never have. Not for a single second. That's why I want to work as much as I can. To have my own life. My own money. I don't want to settle for anyone, despite how much my parents try to tell me I should."

After she yawned widely, I released her and got off the bed. "I'll bring in a tray of food," I said as she watched me go toward the door.

As wonderful as it was to hold her, I felt eager to look into this Elliot Hines. Tessa's parents too. I wasn't sure if she understood how badly I felt this need to take care of her. Killing her rapists was only the start. I wanted to fix everything in her life. She'd become my purpose, and I was impatient to start taking care of her troubles.

When I came back from the kitchen, I found her napping. Instead of lingering to watch over her, I set the tray down on a table and added a simple note:

I'll be back. I wanted her to read it and simply know that I wasn't leaving her.

The guard I positioned at the door would patrol and keep an eye on her. I wasn't worried about her leaving, but I couldn't head off without knowing some security would be here on the lookout.

I went to the mansion to speak with both my father and Franco about this supposed fiancé Tessa didn't want. Or an almost fiancé. Whoever he was, I wanted more information. It made sense to update my father about the fact that I had a woman with me. Not like that… but after holding Tessa on the bed, I knew she wouldn't be going anywhere anytime soon. And not just because she was avoiding going home.

"Did this guy propose to her?" Franco asked after I gave them the basics.

I'd caught them at a convenient time. Nina was inside, sorting out things for the baby's arrival. Franco and my father were sitting out by the pool at the table we used for meetings.

"No. I don't think so." I rubbed the back of my neck and paced. They'd listened to all that I'd explained already, but Franco wanted to follow up. "She made it sound like Elliot is just someone her parents have always known, and they're trying to persuade her to marry him."

"And she's not interested?" my father asked.

"No. Not at all."

"What firm did you say this guy worked at?" Franco asked again, scrolling on his phone. He was probably already looking him up.

"Elliot Hines. He's a lawyer at J.R.G. firm." I grimaced. "Fuck. His name sounds so damn familiar."

"I agree." Nina walked over the patio, her face pinched with worry.

My father frowned and held his arm out for her to sit in his lap. He never excluded her, even from conversations about business, but she never inserted herself into our serious talks, either.

The fact that she was now, clearly overhearing some of what I said, was suspicious. The windows were all open, so it wasn't as though I'd tried to hide what I was saying. But her expression…

"What's wrong?" I asked her.

"Elliot Hines does sound familiar." She glanced at my father. "It sounds like the creepy asshole my best friend, Tessa West, has been avoiding for years."

Tessa West. I had her full name now. As Nina lowered to sit on my father's thigh, she peered at me. "How did you find her?"

I sighed, hating that I'd need to break the news to her that her friend had been raped. It wasn't my story to tell her. But Tessa could. I wondered why she would tell me that she had no one, and that no one ever helped her, if Nina claimed they were best friends.

"I'll take you to her now, and she can explain."

And she can explain to me how she's friends with my father's fiancée.

It *was* a small world, but I wanted to make sure that Tessa simply stayed in mine, however she might already be connected. Because now that I'd found her, I couldn't imagine letting her go.

8

TESSA

The next time I woke in the same bed that Romeo held me in, I wasn't hit with the instant dread and trepidation. I lay there for several minutes, scanning the room that was already becoming so familiar. Not only did I easily recognize these four walls and the sort-of-hideous striped wallpaper that the seventies wanted back, but I also knew I'd be safe behind the closed door.

Romeo had to be near in this old house, and if he wasn't, he'd come back. He had so far, and I believed him when he said that he wanted to help me. The look in his serious, ice-blue eyes suggested that he wanted to take care of me in every way I needed assistance.

He killed a man—three men—for me.

If that wasn't an ultimate act of going over the top to see to someone's needs, I wasn't sure what else would count. I hadn't realized how much I wanted those men dead, too stuck in the dismay and pain of what they'd done. But the moment I saw the sign of his wounded knuckles from punching someone, I was struck with a need to inflict pain in kind. Or to know that they'd been taken care of.

Danicia warned me that I would be very tired, exhausted down to my bones no matter how much I rested. The emotional turmoil. The survival instinct and running on fumes. That wasn't including how fatigued I was on a normal day just from working myself so hard.

I'd never had a chance to sleep in, always expected to do chores and whatever else my mom and dad asked of me. They never let me rest, and they were judgmental when I wanted to be lazy. "Self-care" was a laughable notion to them.

Here, I could just… be. It couldn't last, but I dared to dream that what those men did to me triggered a turning point in my life.

I yawned as the last threads of sleepiness left me, and I got up to go to the bathroom. On the way there, I spotted the tray of food. A note had been added, and I stared at the sharp penmanship of Romeo's message.

I'll be back.

-R

I set the note down, glad that he'd given me an indication of his pending return.

See? He will *be back.* I didn't have to worry about being left here or stranded.

Using the shower, I grimaced at the signs of wear and tear in the small room. While my standards were low, *really* low to the degree that I was super easy to please, I wondered if this huge house was under renovation. As I cleaned up, careful with my wounds, I envisioned how nice this place could look. New paint and hardware. Remove the chipped and stained tiles. A more up-to-date window with a screen. Even the décor. It all needed fixing or replacing, and mentally redecorating and renovating gave me an escape from reality. Once I was done, I applied all the creams that Danicia left. They went a long way in soothing my stinging flesh.

Back in the room, I smiled at the neat pile of clothes left on a chair.

Romeo asked that I come back today and check on your vitals. (All good.) I didn't want to wake you. You need all the rest you can get. These clothes are extras, in case you need something to change into. If you need ANYTHING, don't hesitate to call me.

-Danicia

She really went above and beyond. While it should've alarmed me that she came in the room without my knowledge, it wasn't any different than if I'd gone to the hospital and the shift nurse came on a vitals check. I appreciated it, and I hurried to put on the yoga pants and shirt that seemed closest to my size. The garments were a bit baggy, but it was good enough.

I left my room to find Romeo, hoping for a chance to tell him how grateful I was for Danicia's help. It might not have seemed like a lot to him, but these displays of consideration were extravagant gifts, in my opinion.

"Romeo?"

I knew a guard had to be near. Romeo and Danicia mentioned one being stationed here. It made me curious—again—as to what organization Romeo worked for. A deadly one. But not law enforcement? He had a funny expression on his face when I asked if he was a hitman.

"But isn't he one?" I whispered to myself as I searched through the house. If he killed three men, he had to have hunted them down quickly, then had the strength and know-how to pull off that feat. That meant he had resources of some kind.

Questions for later. The food on the tray had gone cold while I napped, so after I searched the upstairs levels, I headed down to locate the kitchen. Food would make me more clear-headed, and I doubted my stomach could grumble any louder.

Maybe I could make him lunch. I frowned, glancing at my watch. *Uh, maybe an early dinner?* I'd been sleeping so much that my routine was all out of whack.

I found the kitchen and cringed at how dirty and cluttered it was. My guesses seemed accurate. This was no ordinary messiness. It was the chaos of construction—or reconstruction. The house had good bones. I was no expert to know what I was talking about, but I noticed the spaciousness. Homes didn't have such high ceilings like these anymore. And the huge windows let in so much light. Older features like crown moldings and ornate doorframes made me wonder how old this place was, and I smiled at the prospect of seeing it shed its outer shell of neglect and wear and tear to morph into a grand mansion again.

I sighed, looking through the fridge that seemed to have been updated. It wasn't the right size for the nook it was shoved into, but it was new and functioning, offering the makings for a sandwich, at least.

Maybe he put this in so he can live here while it's renovated?

Again, I tried to stem my frustration of having so many questions about Romeo. He looked fit and strong enough to make this a DIY effort of renovation, but I still had no clue who the man really was.

Later. Food now, then when he's back, I'll ask more.

He'd been so gentle, letting me rest, and so giving to hold me without expecting anything at all. For all I didn't know about Romeo, I was fully aware of the qualities that I liked in him so far.

Even the killing part? I cringed a bit as I set out the layers I'd want to make this sandwich complete, but as I turned to put the deli meat into the fridge, I froze.

Outside the windows I'd been admiring, a man crept along a row of hedges.

Fuck! Panic filled me so quickly, I was even faster to hold in a shriek. I'd been pushed onto this adrenaline rush so often lately that I was becoming used to managing it.

Fear didn't root me in place as I stayed paralyzed and unmoving. If I could see him—and the second guy behind him—they could see me. Like a deer caught in the headlights, I held my breath and watched as they snuck along.

Fuck. Fuck. Fuck!

I refused to lose my cool to terror, but I was frightened by their presence. Both of them looked tall, muscled, and grungy in bandanas, leather biker cuts, and raggedy jeans. These were no random trespassers, but members of a motorcycle gang.

What the hell are they *doing here?*

The Devil's Brothers MC was a collection of assholes on bikes. The little I knew of them didn't make me comfortable. They were rumored to traffic women and kids. They were always armed and looking so sinister to use their guns whenever they pleased.

Nina's brother Ricky once bet with the leader, Reaper, at the Hound and Tea's private gambling rooms. Because of that bet, Nina decided to be a Mafia boss's fake girlfriend. The last I'd heard from her was how much she seriously wanted the older man.

Why are they here? What are they doing? I wasn't informed of where the bikers usually terrorized people, but I couldn't understand what they'd want *here.*

Did they see this place looking like a dump and think it's a vacant home to squat in?

Are they just trespassing and looking around for something to do?

I didn't know, but when one stood and held up a knife that dripped with blood, my heart raced faster. Air couldn't enter my lungs fast enough.

That was fresh blood. It was still dripping, and I didn't want to know what or who they'd killed or hurt.

How is this my life? Why is this happening? Questions flogged my mind, but I didn't let them keep me locked up. Without moving all of my body, I extended my arm slowly and steadily. As soon as my fingers wrapped around the hilt of a steak knife wedged in the knife block, I pulled it out and held it tightly.

Keeping my eyes on the men, I inched back toward the wall.

Can they see me in here? Are the windows actually dirty enough that they're not so clear?

Breathing through my nose, I strained not to make a sound. Not to make a big move. If they happened to turn and look through these windows instead of creeping closer to the ones that lined the rear wall of the dining room, I'd be spotted.

Where's the guard? Is there a guard? Where is Romeo?

A silly thought of Shakespeare's famous line rang through my mind.

Where art thou, Romeo? Come on. Focus, Tess!

My thoughts were already scattering from yet another hit of anxiety and panic. I couldn't let myself get hysterical, not now. I had to stay focused, and I tried my best to hide.

Other than that stupid joke, I kept all my attention on the two bikers. If I could reach the wall and sink lower, they wouldn't be able to see me through the windows at all. Then I could crawl back upstairs and lock myself in a room on the highest floor. This knife was the best I could think of as a weapon, but I almost whimpered in my mind at the wishful prayer of Romeo returning soon. He was a killer. He'd know how to defend himself and me in this situation that made no sense.

Already, I'd identified him as a figure of safety, and it was too ironic that he was likely a bad man according to society.

My heel pressed against the wall, and I shook with a deeper breath of relief.

Okay. I've got to be back far enough.

Ever so slowly, watching the men stomping through the overgrown jungle of weeds outside, I dipped toward the floor.

There. I was down, on my knees, ignoring the aches and stings of putting pressure on the skin I'd cut open and bruised when I fell last night. I had to deal with it, and I did, biting the inside of my cheek to distract myself from the pain. I hunched over to crawl away, tucking out of a sight.

A crash sounded outside, and I flinched. Frozen again, I held my breath. My muscles tensed, but I refused to budge. Distant curses reached me, and I thought I heard one biker berating the other for knocking something over.

Okay. Good. It's all good. They're out there. I'm in here, and I'll be safe if I hide. Until Romeo comes back.

Moving over the floor, I tried to reach the stairs. It was a vulnerable pass, exposed between the kitchen and the stairwell. This house was so big, this foyer was so wide, I'd have to sacrifice being more visible to reach the stairs and go up.

Go, Tess. Go. You can do this. He'll be back. He said he'd be back. So just hang on until—

I was halfway to the stairs when someone pounded on the door.

Fuck!

No!

I scrambled upright, torn with the urgency to run up the stairs or hook the deadbolt on the door.

The doorknob twisted, and as I heard the metal of the door's hardware click, I pushed to stand. Then I lunged at the door, hoping my awkward hold on this puny steak knife would maim whoever was breaking in. Romeo wouldn't knock. It had to be one of the bikers, coming to hurt me with the bloody blade I saw.

As the door flung open, I screamed and lifted the steak knife.

A slim arm raised to deflect my strike as I braced to slam my hand down. I'd sink this weapon into whoever dared to threaten me. No matter how hard I'd have to fight.

But a familiar voice yelled out.

The face staring back at me wasn't one of the bikers.

Nina stood there, wide-eyed and terrified as she crouched from my coming hit. "Don't!"

9

ROMEO

"Get back!" My father shoved me aside as he stepped forward to pull Nina into a protective hold. Turning, he gave Tessa his back.

She screamed in response to seeing Nina at the front door, though, and with a jerky shift to the side, she lowered the steak knife before it hit anyone.

We crowded at the door, my father, Nina, Franco, and I. But I pushed closer to both take the knife out of Tessa's hand and hug her.

"Tess!" I said, shortening her name and raising my voice to cut through the utter panic clouding in her eyes. She was terrified, breathing so fast. And alarmed as she stared at Nina still held back by my father. He glared at Tessa, not trusting her with that welcome.

"Nina?" Tessa asked from my embrace. "Is it really you?" With a slight shake of her head, she gasped before Nina could speak. "Hurry!"

Now she pulled at me, forcing me inside with haste. Franco was on alert, staring at her, then scanning our surroundings. She seemed to be wary of something, prompting us with grabby hands to tug us into the house. Franco wasn't our best capo for the hell of it. He was quick to realize she was scared for us standing out here.

"There's a man." She sniffled and inhaled deeply. "Two men. Bikers." She frantically pointed out the door with a trembling finger as she pulled at my arm to get me inside.

"What?" My father lost his skepticism of Tessa as he joined Franco in looking around. "Bikers?"

"Oh, fuck." Nina lurched toward Tessa and wrapped her in a hug, backing away from the door. I pulled my gun free, as did my father and Franco. "You're sure?"

"Who—"

Tessa cut off my father. "Bikers from that club. The Devil's Brothers." She shot a worried look at me. "I saw them out the kitchen window and I thought—"

I squeezed her hand. "Stay here."

Nina nodded at me as Tessa watched me.

"Be careful!"

Her words would be heeded. I was always careful in this dangerous lifestyle.

"Stay in here," I repeated as I hurried out the door with my father and Franco. "Don't come outside until we're back."

Tessa grabbed my hand, furrowing her brow. "He's got a knife."

I responded to that by picking up the steak knife she'd dropped and handing it to her. "Stay inside."

Then I ran out with the other two.

"I thought you had Joseph patrolling here," Franco said as we checked the perimeter of the house.

We all searched for him and the two bikers Tessa claimed to see. I believed her. She wouldn't have gone to the extremes of using a knife for anything but defense. The fear in her eyes wasn't an act.

"He was." I hadn't asked more than one man to guard the place because it wasn't one of the properties anyone ever visited or stayed at. I'd only just started this process of renovating it as my project.

"What the fuck are those bastards doing here?" my father demanded.

I doubted his whispered growl was something he expected Franco or me to answer. It was rhetorical and full of anger, instead.

"I don't see how they could've followed me here," I said. I'd only brought Tessa here recently. And I didn't have a large presence of a Constella force coming and going. Only Danicia. Franco. Joseph, and me. That was it.

"They're getting bolder," my father said. "When I told them we'd wage war against them, I counted on them to strike first after we killed their men at their clubhouse."

Which means we already have hit them first. I grunted as we trekked around the house, looking near and far for the slightest disturbance in the weeds to give us a clue of where someone could have gone. The further we went from the house, I regretted not staying back with the women. Tessa and Nina would be vulnerable if the bikers went toward the building.

Before I could suggest that we circle back and one of us stay, the roar of engines rose in the distance. One by one, the two motorcycles revved up loudly and then faded as they sped off.

"Dammit." I lowered my arm, resting my gun at my side as we completed a full circuit around the house.

"She said she saw them where?" Franco asked.

"The kitchen windows," I replied, leading them back toward that wall.

"They know we're watching them," Franco said as we looked around the area where Tessa spotted the men. "Even though our spies are hiding the best they can, those bastards have to know that we're preparing to annihilate them."

"Them and the Giovannis," I added.

My father sighed heavily, stressed and bothered about this development of the Devil's Brothers here and snooping on me. I was his son, the prince to his leadership. That position made me a target, so it was telling that they'd try to spy on me versus anyone else in the family.

"I hate this waiting around," my father groused. "The stalling and preparing."

"Better than rushing out and slaughtering them carelessly," I said unnecessarily. He knew that. He'd been a leader for decades. Yet that was the simple reason we had to be patient. The Devil's Brothers were new to the criminal scene, but they had many members. They, with Stefan Giovanni's help, wouldn't be easy to eradicate.

"Fuck," Franco said as he hurried into the tall grass near the beginning of the brush.

We jogged with him, staying together as a team. My father was the next to swear. "Mother fuckers!"

Joseph lay in the grass. Blood spilled from a gash over his neck as well as a hole in his chest. Those bikers had killed him.

I locked down, letting my anger surge through me. Another man was down. Another brother had been killed.

Fury clouded my mind, severing any logic that could keep me in the moment.

We lived a dangerous life. We were men who were motivated to judge and serve with violence. Death was inevitable, but so soon after the loss of the three soldiers I'd supervised and led in the meeting with the now-defunct Domino Family, I hated the thought of failing again.

I'd asked Joseph to guard this property while I went to speak with my father and Franco about Elliot Hines. I'd stationed the man here, assuming nothing would come near Tessa at this house not many knew about.

Indirectly, I'd set him up to die. All the Constella men were trained and resourced with a means to kill, but two bikers sneaking up on one man didn't present good odds.

Not again.

I rubbed my hand over my face, letting my fury sink in and spread through me more evenly.

Not fucking again.

It was ludicrous to ever think this would stop. As long as the Constella name reigned supreme in New York, all of us in the family would have limited mortality.

But it was simply too soon. I hadn't yet gotten a decent grip on the survivor's guilt from losing the trio of soldiers earlier this summer. And seeing Joseph killed on the job—the assignment I put him on—was like a punch to the gut, shattering my conscience again.

"Son of a bitch," Franco said as he needlessly checked Joseph's pulse. Just in case, on the rare chance that he hadn't bled out.

"No more waiting," my father vowed, looking down at the soldier who'd died for the family. "The wait is over. They came here, onto our territory, and killed one of ours." He lifted his serious, angry gaze to meet mine, then Franco's. "And now we will go after theirs."

"We won't stop until we've killed them all." I knew that down to my bones, in the depth of my cold heart. It filled me with a renewed sense of urgency, of determination. Not guilt.

"Go," Franco urged, already calling another man out to help handle Joseph's body. "Go back to the women," he told me, then my father.

Franco was a capo, but just because we were the two top leaders of the organization didn't mean that he would hesitate to instruct us.

My father was stuck staring at Joseph, livid that the bikers came here. I managed to look away, sending a silent thanks to the sacrifice he made in keeping Tessa safe until his last breath. Tessa, who still needed to be safe. Nina as well. Franco was right to tell us to go back to the house and be near them, but we'd heard the bikes roar off into the distance. I doubted more were around.

"I'll have more of a crew come here to help with more adequate security," Franco said, "now that the word is out about this property being your residence for the time being."

My father frowned, holding up his hand. "But were they here for him?"

Huh? "Who else could they be here for?"

"The woman. Tessa." He looked from me to Franco, waiting for a reply. When we didn't speak up, he added, "Is there a chance they're out here looking for her?"

I shook my head. "I doubt it. She was just a waitress, no ties to anyone of any organization until I ran into her."

Franco gaped at me. "Wait. What the hell does that mean? One look at her and you're... you're claiming her as yours?"

That was way too far to predict right now. "I mean she's connected to me—so far—because I took her under my direct protection. I tasked Andy with finding her rapists, and I killed them last night."

My father rubbed his face. "That's basically marking her as yours."

I'd skimmed over the part about her being raped when I spoke with them earlier. I wanted to focus on this tie with Elliot Hines and why he sounded familiar. That conversation hadn't been concluded, either, because as soon as Nina overheard his name and guessed that the

Tessa I found was her best friend whom she'd lost contact with, we hurried over here.

Only to find a couple of bikers lurking around.

"Well, wait a second," I said. "They came here when I was gone. If they were waiting for me to go to trespass, maybe they were after Tessa?"

Franco shrugged while my father nodded, as though he approved of my jumping on his train of thought.

"Or," Franco argued, "they noticed you coming and going and wanted to wait until you arrived."

"That makes sense, too. When we rescued Nina from their clubhouse, we killed two of Reaper's top men," my father said. "I could see Reaper wanting to strike back in kind, taking out one of my top men."

Meaning us. Franco and I shared a glance while he waited for his call to pick up.

"Don't send security out here," my father ordered. Looking at me, he exhaled a long breath. "You need to relocate. Clearly, they wanted something out here. A chance to hit you. Or this girl you found."

Franco nodded. "It could just be that the Constella forces are spying on them more and they don't like it."

"Tough shit," I replied.

"I don't want war," my father said. "Not with a baby on the way and settling Nina into our new lives. But if they escalate this any further, if they encroach any closer, the time to spy and collect intel is over. We will fight to the death defending what is ours."

And we will be the victors in any war we engage in. Confidence, not cockiness, had me convinced of it.

"Weston?" Franco asked once a soldier answered his call. "I need you to grab your crew and come my way."

My father and I turned, leaving Franco with Joseph's body. As we walked back toward the house, I considered what I would need to do next. Keeping Tessa safe was paramount. I hated to see her so scared, but I felt a bit of relief with the knowledge that she wasn't helpless. She wasn't naïve and so stunned that she couldn't think of defending herself. That steak knife wouldn't have helped much, but it was the principle of it. She was in a mode to survive.

"You intend to keep her?" my father asked.

"Tessa?"

"Who the fuck else would I be talking about?" he shot back with plenty of impatient sarcasm.

"I do." Sometime during the moments I held her on that bed, the realization hit hard. I did want to keep Tessa with me, but that was no simple quest.

"Is it like Franco guessed? One look at her and that's it?"

If he was asking me about my opinions of love at first sight, I was inclined to reply with an affirmative. Love seemed like a stretch. Tessa and I had only known each other for almost one whole day. It was likely far, far too soon for a complex connection like love, but the concern I felt for her was no petty, temporary care.

"It might be," I replied, hedging on the complete truth.

The thought of sending Tessa away wasn't one I wanted to hold for long. Being near her felt right. Even though she was still acclimating to the post-trauma phase of what those bastards did to her, she seemed drawn to me, not repulsed or pushed away.

10

TESSA

"That's Dante?" I whispered as Nina and I tucked into my room upstairs. I locked the door as she ran to the window to look out it.

"Yes," she replied, just as shaken up as I was. Our reunion was unexpected and swift, but we were both too wrapped up in fear to really do more than hurry to safety.

"Damn." I shook my head, joining her at the window to look out over the weedy lawn. It was extensive, but so thick with grasses and vines from the lack of maintenance from long ago. Multiple seasons, at least. I held my breath as the three men stalked carefully through the yard, looking out for danger.

Nina exhaled a long breath, and I hated the fatigue in it. "I'm sorry." I winced as I faced her profile, stunned by how healthy and happy she looked. The last I saw of her was at the Hound and Tea, when we'd joked about finding a sugar daddy to make our lives easier. She had, sort of. Dante was at least twenty years older than her. Before she met him and agreed to pretend to be his girlfriend, the tiredness in her eyes made her look haggard and beaten down, just like me.

Now, she was glowing. No bags under her eyes. Less of that constant stress lining her face. And... thicker? She seemed to have put on weight. Or maybe her dress made her boobs look that much bigger. *Of all the things to notice, Tess...*

"I'm sorry I almost stabbed you. I thought it was the bikers coming to the door and..."

She placed her arm around my shoulders and pulled me close in a side hug. "Don't apologize for being scared."

"I wouldn't have hurt you," I said anyway.

"I know. I know."

"But I *was* shocked as hell to see you show up here. What's going on? Why's Dante here and..." I shook my head as we both still peered out the window. "Why are you here with Romeo?" It had been one shock after another. Seeing the Devil's Brothers. Then Nina showing up. The worry that I could've hurt her in my fear.

"Did Romeo tell you who he is?" she asked carefully, giving up her post to glance at me.

"No. Just that his name is Romeo. He works for an organization and he..." I dragged in a deep breath, determined to plow ahead and really catch her up since I'd lost touch with her. That meant coming out with the full truth. "And he killed the three men who raped me last night."

She lost all focus on staring out the window. Her worry about Dante couldn't have disappeared, but she turned her full, anxious attention to me. "*What?*" She gaped at me and shook her head. "No. You didn't just say..."

I nodded, showing her my bandaged hands. "I was waitressing late, and after my shift, these men chased me down the alley and..."

Her arms clenched around me so tightly, I choked for air. I hugged her back, sniffling at the familiar burn of tears threatening to spill. I'd missed her, so damn much. Being near her again, regardless of the confusing details I still wanted to piece together, felt good. It felt right to be reunited with my best friend, the sister I'd always wanted. When no one else would ever stand up for me, Nina was there, supporting me however she could with her equally limited power and resources.

"Okay." I reared back as she wiped at her cheeks, crying for what I'd shared. "*What* is going on?"

First, I'd noticed her boobs practically spilling out. But now, with that hug, I knew I wasn't imagining the bump in her belly. "Are you *pregnant?*" It was my turn to gape at her.

She nodded, trading in the teary frown at the news that I'd been raped for a slight smile. "Yes. Dante and I are expecting our baby in the spring."

"Oh, my God!" I hauled her in for another hug. "We have so much to catch up on."

"We do. And we definitely will. Because you're not going anywhere."

I huffed a laugh. I wasn't prepared to make any predictions or plans for myself. She was pregnant! I was still so stunned that I didn't know what to say.

"Because Romeo is Dante's son, Tess. That's why I'm here. He said he found a woman and helped her out of a situation last night."

I pointed at myself. "That'd be me." I was impressed—and pleased—that he hadn't told them I was raped.

"I was eavesdropping on what he was telling Dante and Franco." At my confused look, she added, "Franco is the man with them out there. I was in the house and heard bits and pieces of what Romeo was talking about, that a woman needed help, and he rushed to help her. Then when he said this woman was afraid of some guy named Elliot Hines, I knew he had to be talking about you!"

I nodded. "Romeo brought me here and had a 'friend' named Danicia check me over."

She grinned. "Danicia is so helpful. She was on vacation when I learned I was pregnant, but she's been so helpful and comforting."

"When he brought me here, I was, um, struggling with processing what happened. I guess I blurted out that no one—that Elliot—wouldn't want me since I was damaged goods…"

I swallowed hard. It was still so hard to say it.

"Well, Romeo was curious about who he was. It seems like Romeo and the others might know a little about Elliot and some of his cases."

"But who *are* they, Nina? Who does Romeo work for?" As soon as the words left me, her earlier comment replayed in my mind. It was so much to catch up with that I failed to react sooner.

"Because Romeo is Dante's son."

"The *Mafia*?" I hissed. Romeo was involved with the Constella Family, one of the cornerstone organizations of the syndicated crime world. Not only was he included in their ranks, but he also had to be high up if he was the son of Dante—the boss.

Now that she was in front of me, present and communicating after the month of no contact, more and more clicked. She'd mentioned Romeo in her calls before I lost touch with her. Or she'd hinted at Dante having a son. Never in a million years, though, did I think we'd meet like this. That my best friend was dating the father of the man who'd rescued me, who'd killed for me.

"Wow." I blinked quickly, shaking my head with this stupefied sense of surprise.

"He's Dante's son," she repeated. "Romeo is like a prince of the Mafia."

I shot her a look. "Jesus. Mafia royalty? That's a thing?"

"I don't know. But Dante more or less declared that war would be coming when his old friend Stefan teamed up with the Devil's Brothers to kidnap me."

I gawked at her again. I was raped. She'd been kidnapped. We needed to talk for hours.

"Yeah, it's complicated. But I'm safe. Dante and I are engaged. We're having a baby. Romeo's protecting you. We will be safe." She backed up the promise by grabbing my hands and squeezing them without touching the bandages.

"Don't..." She winced and studied me. "Don't let these labels intimidate you. The knowledge that Dante and Romeo are Mafia men. They are *good* men."

I held up my hand. "No. No. I'm not..." I sighed, hoping I could explain. "I'm not worried about Romeo being in the Mafia. I'm not scared of him." I loved her all the more for rushing to console me, but it wasn't necessary. "Somehow, I know he won't hurt me."

She whooshed out a deep breath of relief and hugged me again. It seemed like she couldn't get enough of holding me close, as though she needed to make up for all the lost time.

I wasn't nervous about Romeo. I wasn't scared of him. He wasn't a threat. I knew that from the bottom of my heart, and I didn't care how quickly that idea had settled in. It was a fact. I felt safer when he was near. I felt stronger and supported when he was within reach. I wondered if it was a sign of an attachment issue, an instant sense of hero worship because he'd saved me from those men and then killed them for what they did to me.

And if I am falling under some spell or suffering from an attachment issue...

I wouldn't want it any other way. Being near or connected to that sexy, tatted Mafia prince didn't sound like a bad thing at all.

"I kept texting you and calling you," Nina said as the front door opened downstairs.

"Tess?" Romeo called up.

I smiled quickly, liking how he shortened my name. "Up here."

"It's all clear," Dante yelled up to us.

Nina and I left the room to meet up with them, but she didn't stay quiet. "I kept calling and texting you. I was so worried when you didn't reply."

I frowned at her. "Me too. I kept texting and had no clue why you went AWOL on me."

"Huh." She scrunched her face. "I'll ask Dante to have someone look into it. I got a new phone because mine was so old that it broke, but the number is the same." She shook her head. "I got scared that your parents or Elliot coerced you into an elopement and I'd never hear from you again."

I took her hand and squeezed it as we walked down the stairs. "Never. We're best friends for life."

Seeing her grin at me was the reward I didn't know I'd needed.

But spotting Romeo down in the foyer felt just as good. In a different way.

Attachment issues or not, I lit up at his presence.

"We've got to move," he announced, looking me over as if he was worried I'd been hurt, not just scared. "The MC knows I'm here, and it's no longer safe."

"What about the guard?" I asked, feeling stupid to mention it.

"They killed him," Dante said as Nina went to him. "You need more security, and this place won't be easy to patrol with the state that the property is in."

All those weeds sure would make it easy to hide.

"Franco is arranging for more men to help as a security force," Dante said, "but it's unwise to stay here."

"But what does this mean?" I locked onto Romeo's ice-blue eyes.

"It means I'm taking Nina home. Now," Dante told us as he focused on my friend. "We can talk later." When he looked at me, then Romeo, he said, "You can remain under the protection of the Constella forces, Tessa. It's up to you where you'd want to go."

"The family has—" Romeo stopped, looking between me and Nina. "Did she fill you in? That I'm Romeo Constella and he's…" He gestured at Dante.

I nodded. "The boss of the Constella Mafia."

"I started to catch her up on what's happened since we worked together at the Hound and Tea," Nina replied.

Romeo faced me. "The family has multiple properties. I'd planned to stay here for a while and renovate this place, but I'll move to another location after Joseph was attacked."

"Romeo has been supervising surveillance on our enemies," Dante said, full of authority, "and with this incident today, he will increase his effort in that regard."

Please, please don't expect me to leave him. I licked my lips, nervous as I watched Romeo stand there so serious and quiet, patient and open to listening to what I could decide.

The distance between us in this foyer felt too wide and far. The mere thought of being away from him hurt me. It tore at my mind and chipped at my vulnerable heart.

"Do you want to stay with me?" he asked.

I nodded, running toward him.

He held his arms open, and once I reached him, secure against his hard chest and hearing his heart beat steadily, I sighed with the basic and simple relief of knowing I was back where I thought I belonged.

With you.

11

ROMEO

"We need to go right now?" Tessa asked me.

"Yes." I looked down into her dark-blue gaze, captivated all over again at the depth of trust that shone there. Nina and Tessa both confirmed that the truth was out about me. Tessa now knew that I was involved with the Mafia.

If learning that I'd killed those three men hadn't scared her away, I worried that revealing my connection and importance to a Mafia organization might.

No worries there. So far. She'd run into my arms. That was a high sign that she wanted to be near me, not distance herself.

"We will stay in touch," Nina promised. She reached out to grab Tessa's hand and squeezed it, and I was damned glad that the blonde stayed tucked at my side. I didn't see any reason to lower my arm, and keeping her close felt natural.

"I'll ask Dante and Franco about our phones and whatnot." Nina glanced at me as my father led her out the door. "Now that I know you're with Romeo, I can reach you one way or another."

"Yes. I feel like we've only begun to scratch the surface of catching up, mama-to-be."

Nina's smile was sweet and sincere, but she didn't dally and try to linger with her best friend she'd only just gotten reacquainted with.

Once she was out the door, I caught my father's eye and nodded at him. Before we came to the house, I told him that I'd move to a vacation house that wasn't even under the Constella name. Most properties were hidden with shell corps showing as owners, but this one further out of the city was layered even further from discovery, willed to one of the old-timers who'd passed away several years ago. Like this house, the cabin had been sitting and neglected. The main perk about the place was the extensive network of surveillance cameras and tech capacity that could be started up again. Franco likely had already sent someone to hook it up and test it before I'd get there.

Before we *would get there.*

Alone with Tessa again, I felt the need to tread carefully. I couldn't expect her to just give up her life and follow me. Everything felt tenuous and delicate, but I wanted to forge a path forward with her. "I understand that this is a big request, to relocate with me…"

She shook her head and stepped back. "But I want to go with you." When she lowered her gaze, worry returned, but she faced me again. "If you want me to come with you."

"Yes. I told you that I'd help you, Tessa, and that means lying low with me until you figure out what you want to do next, so that's what we'll do."

She smiled slightly. "Thank you."

"But I understand that you had a life before I found you. A job—"

She scoffed. "Which one? The bar I left last night? My shift started an hour ago and that's my first no-call, no-show. I'm fired."

I frowned, not liking the resignation in her voice.

"The Hound and Tea?" She arched one brow. "Now that I know you're a Constella and the owner of that steakhouse, I guess you could give me a sabbatical from waitressing there."

I nodded, not relaxed enough to smile yet, but she had good points. "And you're certain your parents won't wonder…"

"I bet they're pissed that I've gone missing, wondering where I am, but *angry*, not *worried* about it." She crossed her arms, smirking. "I'm guessing my dad went to get his car, and that's it."

"No one else who'd notice you missing and report it or anything?"

She started to shake her head but stopped midway. "I guess Elliot would be curious, but he's not *my* concern. I don't care what he thinks or guesses."

I liked the sound of that. Even though there were more pressing things on hand now, like the Devil's Brothers trespassing on Constella property and killing one of our guards, I didn't intend to give up on figuring out how I could help Tessa with this crooked lawyer she had no interest in.

"We'll head out to the other location now. And once things settle down," I promised as I looked her directly in the eye, "I will resume working on how to sever any obligations or connections you have with Elliot."

She stared at me, seeming to search my face. For what, I didn't know, but I hated the possibility that she might not believe me.

"If that's what you want," I added.

She huffed a light laugh. "Oh, I want. Not having to even think about being with Elliot would be a dream come true." Furrowing her brow, she seemed to rethink her words. "I don't mean… I'm saying… You…"

I raised my brows.

"I'm not asking you to, um, remove him for me." She rubbed her jaw, sheepish now. "Not like you removed those three men last night."

But it'd be my fucking pleasure to. "Killing Elliot Hines would be a different endeavor from killing those three bastards last night. Hines would be missed, and with the connections he seems to have by representing some of our rivals, it would be a complicated mess."

She nodded.

"However," I said and stepped closer, "I *will* do anything and everything to help you and keep you safe, Tess."

Her smile was slow and sexy. "I like when you do that."

"What?" I'd do it again to get that smile.

"Shorten my name. I always wished more people would. I like the sound of it better."

"I like it too, Tess." *And I definitely like what you and I could be if you lower your guard to do more than let me take care of your safety.*

An hour later, we were packed and heading out of the house. A soldier followed us in another car. It had to be the backup security Franco arranged for after Joseph was killed.

Tessa didn't talk on the ride, but I was aware of her looking out the window and watching me through her peripheral vision. The silence wasn't awkward, but I wanted to make sure that she'd didn't spiral or fall back to a quieter, shell-shocked numbness.

What she went through wouldn't—and shouldn't—be dismissed. Trauma is a difficult thing to manage, and I had a suspicion she'd never faced anything like it before. My method of dealing with trauma or anything heavy was to hide my emotions and let a high and thick wall block me from anything else impacting me. It wasn't the healthiest coping mechanism. I knew it was a terrible flaw, but even worse, right now, I felt clueless and inadequate to know how to help Tessa cope.

"I can still contact Danicia if you need her help," I said.

She flinched, and I realized neither of us had spoken for at least a half hour.

"Okay. I don't think you need to ask her to drive far or anything like that. I packed all the clothes she dropped off, and all the medicine."

"Good." God, I hated how stilted I sounded. I wasn't sure how to read her when she acted like everything was fine. There was no way she'd moved on past her trauma yet, so I had to assume she was either ignoring it and shoving it aside or trying to mask how it controlled her, that fake, stoic attempt like I did.

It was easier when she asked me for help. I knew how to care for her when she requested that I hold her. I wasn't confused when she ran toward me to be in my embrace. Maybe it was the distance in the car, the center console separating us as though it were a ten-foot-high wall. But I dreaded that she might be trying to shelter herself from needing anything from me.

If she's determined to be aloof and shut me out, then why would she say she wanted to stick around with me?

By the time we reached the cabin, I was more confused, on edge to be alone with her here.

What if she'd be better off with Nina, someone she knows and cares about?

What if she needs meds or counseling that I can't help with?

What if she changes her mind about leaning on a Mafia prince for protection?

What if—

"I can take the couch," she protested, again, in the living room of the cabin.

"No." I'd told her that plain and simple answer three times now.

"I'm just saying. You're so tall and... and..." She frowned, gesturing at me. "Big. I'm petite and short. I'd fit better on the couch, whereas you'd fit well on the bed."

I shook my head. The only way I'd compromise on those assigned sleeping arrangements was if I shared the bed with her.

Pushing her would be wrong. Until I could better gauge how she was feeling and coping, I couldn't insist on anything from her. It had to be her reaching out to me. It had to be her signal that she wanted to be held again—or anything else.

For the next few days, we settled into a routine. I stayed busy on my laptop, searching through all the intel that came in from our spies. I spent a significant amount of time on the phone with Andy. Then my father. Then Franco. Plus other spies. After the Devil's Brothers dared to set foot on my land, the stakes were higher. Tensions were raised. It was still a waiting game of wondering who'd strike next. We wouldn't until we were ready, because nothing good came from being rash with enemies like those biker bastards and the devious Giovannis.

Trying to give all my attention to preparing to fight our enemies had become my project, and every moment I spent working was one more method of trying to rise above the pressure building between me and Tessa.

She wasn't idle either, on the phone—a new one my father sent here—with Nina. Or she read the e-reader app on the device. When she wasn't doing that, she set herself to giving this dated, dusty cabin a very thorough, deep clean.

"You don't have to," I scolded her the first time she set up to clean.

"I *want* to." She shrugged. "It's how I was raised."

I scoffed. "To be an obedient, good girl?"

She sighed. "Basically. But I like things tidy, too. It's rewarding to clean something up and see it sparkle."

Her hangup with being an "obedient, good girl" was something I intended to revisit later, but I left her to it. Whatever made her happy, and if dusting and mopping satisfied her, I wouldn't stand in her way.

Before long, I realized we'd fallen into a roommate sort of situation. While I wouldn't say she grew more distant, she seemed less likely to strike up a conversation or look my way. At first, I thought she was nervous about interrupting my calls. I told her that she was my priority too, and she waved that comment off.

I was stuck between not wanting to push but desperate to reach her and know that she was coping and recovering, not hiding how much she still suffered. I Had no idea how to achieve that fundamental closeness I'd felt when sitting on the bed with her at the other place.

On the fourth night, I finally got a hint of how poorly she was coping. It came in the middle of the night, when the rain from the evening's storm passed through with a steadier pattern on the roof.

Earlier, the deluge pounded the cabin so hard that the thrum of precipitation cut out all other noises. I got up to check on Tessa, making sure she could sleep through it. And she was fine, dozing deeply. I returned to the small couch, hating that I was stuck with this distance between us.

Why won't she reach out to me again? Ever since she learned that I was in the Mafia, she was staying away. She seemed so determined to appear strong, not needing anything from me, but I refused to be duped that easily.

The cry that came from her room suggested otherwise, that she was scared and feeling hopeless. If she was scared of storms, I'd comfort her. I was over the top, smitten and obsessed with this woman, but it didn't stop me from checking on her.

"Tess?" I loved the nickname she preferred. "Tess?"

I entered the only bedroom where she slept. In the darkness, I made out the shape of her alone on the bed. Crying. Whimpering.

Fuck. I hated to see her distraught.

"Tessa?"

Shit. It looked like she was dreaming. A nightmare, judging by the tight features of her strained face and the tears on her cheeks.

Tess. I swallowed past the emotions clogging my throat. This woman, still so much a stranger, moved me to struggle with myself. Her happiness would make mine possible.

"Tess, it's me. It's okay. Wake up." I sat on the edge of the bed, brushing her hair from her face.

"No. Don't. No! don't let them…" She sobbed harder, and it broke me.

"Tess!" I had to snap her out of this night terror. If she was reliving the rape, I had to break the memories and spare her more pain.

"Tess. It's me. Romeo. Wake up." I shook her harder, digging my thumbs into the smooth skin of her upper arms as I lifted her slightly off the bed. It killed me to witness her distress, trapped in her mind.

"They're coming for me," she mumbled in her sleep.

Fuck that. No one would come after her for the sake of malice ever again.

Only I would be there for her. I would always come to her rescue. And as illogical and backward as it probably seemed as a plan, I reacted with what I was sure could be a sharp jolt to her system and wake her the fuck up.

I leaned down and kissed her, hard.

12

TESSA

A hard push against my mouth startled me. I was yanked straight out of my nightmare from the contact over my lips. I jerked, sucking in a deep inhale through my nose. As I opened my eyes, my heart raced faster. My breaths became more labored. Stuck in this nightly loop of panic and terror, I wasn't sure how much more I could handle.

Romeo's face filled my view. The firm grip of his big hand held the back of my head as he kept us close together. His lips were smashed to mine, and with a click of awareness, of understanding that *he* was *kissing* me, the remnants of my nightmare fell apart. The darkness of reliving that night faded. Shards of the bad dream scattered, giving me full freedom to experience Romeo kissing me.

The act of waking up seemed to jar him, too, because as I returned the pressure, arching up to keep my lips locked against his, he reared back and breathed hard. His hot exhales feathered over my face as he lifted slightly. As he retreated, the force of air so close to my tear-stained cheeks clued me into how badly I was trapped in the depth of those nightmares.

They came every night. Some mornings, I felt more tired than when I went to bed. But never before had I been rescued from them.

My hero. Romeo was my savior in so many ways.

I gazed up at him in the darkness of the room, hoping he could see that truth in my eyes. Shadows fell over us both, but in the dimness of light, the quiet of the fading storm, it seemed like we truly were the only two people in the world.

"Romeo." I couldn't take this silence, this gnawing tension that pushed me to press my lips to his again.

The desperation in my plea was all it took. He growled, lowering until he brushed his mouth over mine again. Insistently. Hungrily. And with so much need. I felt the power in his soft lips parting mine, and as his tongue swept in to taste and explore my mouth, I tilted my head back, letting him show me.

Before he could take his lips from mine again, I lifted my hands and threaded my fingers through his thick, dark hair, so soft and silky, almost delicate, and in such contrast to the rest of him. He was all hard muscles and tight skin, strength and masculinity exuding from him. Beneath him, I felt small and sheltered, so treasured with his touch.

My heart hadn't slowed. I strained to catch my breath without letting him raise his face from mine. Now, it was desire and affection that triggered me to gasp and whimper, to mewl and pant.

Ever so slowly, as he kissed me so thoroughly and lit the fire of wanton need within me, he dragged his hand down, from the back of my head toward my back, then snaking his arm under me. Getting closer, he dipped over me on the bed. He didn't break the kiss. I didn't protest at all. Not his tongue against mine, his lips pressing mine open. I wanted it all.

It was a stark, sharp difference that I clung to for the sake of my sanity and security. In my nightmare, the now-dead trio of men chased me and reached out for me. They grabbed my clothes, their fingers scraping against my flesh. They were the predators, targeting me like prey to violate and discard.

Not once did they come near my face. None of them had tried to kiss me.

But Romeo did.

I didn't know why he was here. I wasn't sure what encouraged him to kiss me while I was sleeping when during the day, he remained distant from me, too busy to make time for talking me out of my fearsome and low moments.

Romeo's mouth remained on mine now, and while I felt so clueless, I clung to his display of affection and intimacy. No matter how hard and brutal his kisses were, like he was starving for me, I relished the grounding experience of knowing I was here with him, now. Not in the past brought to me via nightmares.

As he followed me onto the bed more fully, his knee pressed against mine. It was still tender, the deepest cut from when I tripped, and I hissed instinctively at the press.

He jerked back, breaking the kiss.

"Romeo, no," I begged as he moved to get back and stand again.

"I—"

"Please," I insisted, extending my hand up toward him.

He caught it and pressed a wet kiss to my palm. "I heard you crying and tried to wake you. That's all."

I nodded. "Nightmares of…"

"I figured." Still, he backed up, letting my hand drop as he knelt back to get off the bed.

"No!" He was already standing, too quick for me to reach him, so I kneeled to get more on level with him. "Don't go."

"I won't push you."

"You already did." I took hold of his hand and clutched it tightly. "You pushed me out of that nightmare."

He sighed, looking away as I held his hand. "I did. But I won't push any further."

I tugged him closer, wishing he'd look me in the eye. "Then I will. I'll push myself. Whatever you can give me, Romeo. To help me. You said you'd help me, remember?"

He gazed at me so seriously, I doubted I'd get through to him. "I don't think you're ready to be with a man, Tess. Not so soon, not... Not with me."

Emboldened by the desire he'd stoked in me, I reached for his other hand and guided him to stand as close to the bed as he could. It seemed impulsive and rash, but I wanted to follow this thrill of him grounding me, of showing me, once and for all, that I truly wasn't alone. Since we'd come here, I'd been so determined to stay out of his way. He had calls to handle and things to arrange. He was a busy man, and I hated how it seemed like I was a burden. An obligation.

With that kiss, he showed me that I might have misinterpreted him all along. That just maybe, he wanted me.

"Help me," I begged. "Help me to forget it all. Keep the nightmares away and stay with me." In a brave move, I brought his hand to my chest and kept it over where my heart beat so wildly for him. For more of his hard kisses and hungry eyes.

"Tess..." He sighed, exhaling long and hard. "You don't know what you're asking for."

"I do." I kneeled closer to the edge of the bed, carried away with this frantic need for him. "I'm asking for *you*. For your help to forget what they did."

"I can't erase what they did," he said softly as he lifted his other hand to cup my face.

At the firm stroke of his thumb over my cheek, I shivered. "I just want you to help me stop the memories. To show me how to forget about it for a moment. To help me shove it away."

"How?" he asked, changing his mind as he kissed me. "Tell me what you want."

I cherished the freedom, the example of having control.

"Can you kiss me again?"

He did, framing my face and urging me to loop my arms around him. After several moments of the heated slide of our lips against each other's and the addictive taste of his tongue in my mouth, I struggled to stay upright on my knees. I'd been leaning into him to spare putting the weight on the still-healing scrapes, but we still weren't close enough.

"Can you…" I frowned, pouting as he watched my face.

"What? What do you want?"

I didn't know how to say it, caught in the strange dilemma of wanting him and feeling aroused but afraid to experience anything more.

"I'm…" I furrowed my brow, wishing he could read my mind. The sensations were too much to handle, and while I wanted to ask him to help me find relief, it was a huge step for me to take.

My pussy throbbed. My nipples felt so hard and achy. Aroused and slick with my juices, I felt… dirty, somehow.

"I was…" I winced. "I was a virgin before those men. And I don't… I've never…"

He kissed me slowly and took my hand. Twisting so I held his fingers, he paused in his kisses long enough to whisper, "Show me. Show me what you want."

I shivered and let his warm, hungry mouth distract me as I brought his hand to my pussy. Angled with my knees apart, I guided him to put his fingers over the achy spot where I felt so needy.

"You're sure?" he checked.

"Please. I just want to forget it all."

He wrapped his arm around me, and in a hug, he followed me down to the bed. Once his muscled form hovered over me, he reared back to pull his shirt off. Nervous, but swept away with this foreign and needy drug of lust, I arched my back to indicate that I wanted him to remove my shirt too.

"Kiss me," I urged when he lowered his hands to remove my panties. As long as I had his lips on mine, I would know he wanted me and treasured this moment.

Together, we took each other's garments off. Once his hot, naked body lay flush to mine, a stubborn intrigue prompted me to be braver yet, to go for what *I* wanted with this man who refused to push me into anything.

I tucked my hand between us as we made out, sloppy kisses and needy tongues and all. The second I slid my fingers down his chiseled abs and touched my fingertips to his hard dick, he tensed.

I pulled back. "Sorry—"

"No." He kissed me harder. "I like it, Tess. I've thought about you touching me every fucking minute of the day."

His words filled me with determination and proof that this had to be right. That he had to be okay with my clumsy exploration.

"Touch me wherever you want. I'm yours, however you want me," he said between presses of his lips on my neck.

"I want you here," I told him as I stroked his hard shaft. Pushing my hips toward him, I hoped that he got the hint. I didn't want to say it. I couldn't. I wouldn't risk making any connection to the last time someone had touched me there, and I wanted him to make this a new memory that I would keep forever.

"Like this?" He angled himself closer, rubbing his dick over my entrance. Each time he ground over me, putting pressure on my clit, I moaned and arched toward him.

"Yes. Please, Romeo. Help me." I was determined to go for it, to shed the fear of my past. Lining him up to my pussy, I widened my legs and welcomed him in.

"Easy," he cautioned, kissing me as he pushed lower and bore more of his weight on me. Slanting over me, he secured our hips together. "Slowly."

I nodded as he pushed inside, just the tip. Already, the stretch was so intense, and I sucked in a sharp breath at the sensation of him opening me up.

He stopped, kissing me and bracing himself over me. Waiting. Teasing. His mouth was too masterful, too wicked for me to allow any fear into my mind, to permit any thought of anyone else to invade on this moment.

"More, Romeo. I want more."

Inch by inch, he pushed into me, pulling out with every thrust. Back and forth, he worked his big, hard cock inside me with a gradual drive. Only once he was seated all the way in me did he groan and wait again, still and catching his breath.

"Are you all right?" he asked, kissing along my jaw and brushing my hair back from my face.

"I'm so full." And the stretch, the fullness, and the pressure urged me to want him to move again.

"But are you all right?"

I shook my head and arched my back. "I need you to move. Please."

His roguish smile was kind and gentle, and I locked onto the promise in his eyes. "Like this?" Thrusting in and out, he dragged his long length over my sensitive walls that sucked him in so hungrily.

"Oh, God. Yes. Romeo!" I cried out as he sped up, but he silenced me with his demanding lips covering mine again. His tongue slid into my mouth in sync with his dick easing into my pussy. Between both actions and the glorious weight of his powerful body rubbing against mine and pinning me to the mattress, I was urged closer and closer to coming.

My orgasm built swiftly, but strongly, and before I could realize what that increasing tension signified, I felt like a band had snapped. Like my nerves were fried and frazzled. Moaning into his mouth as he kissed me without pause, I savored the responding tension in him. He jerked into me harder, growling deeply. Despite the waves of pleasure that radiated from our union, I was still with it and cognizant of him jerking deep inside me, filling me with his hot cum.

"Fuck, Tess. Fuck me. Fuck." He growled and cursed, almost seeming lost in his scattered thoughts and panted claims.

Holding him close, I caught my breath, too stunned and sated with that orgasm to try to speak. He rested his forehead on my temple, and eventually, he lessened the hold of his arms on the bed.

Crushing his weight to me, he blanketed me and completed the act of making me forget. All I could think of or feel was him. All I could relish was that he'd had sex with me and filled me so well. He *had* erased the ugliness of my nightmare, and now, on cloud nine and floating from the pleasure of coming with him, I wanted him to star in all my dreams of the future.

He rolled, hugging me so that I lay draped over him. Entwined and stuck together, we lay there until I was close to drifting off to sleep.

"Let me clean you up," he said, gently urging me to move.

I was too sluggish and comfortable to register anything more than sliding over and snuggling back on the bed. He came back, wiping at me so softly and tenderly. Then when he climbed back onto the bed, I smiled and welcomed his arms wrapping around me, content to lie in his hold in case any bad dreams dared to return.

13

ROMEO

The last time I had such simple, vanilla sex was probably when I was a teen and figuring out what I liked, at least fifteen years ago. Since then, I preferred harder sex. I had kinks and enjoyed being dominant, extremes and all.

When I woke with Tessa in my arms, soft and so relaxed as she slept in, I considered that I'd given her what she'd wanted and asked for but held back from taking what *I* wanted in return.

I was unsatisfied in the sense that I wanted to fuck her hard and leave my mark on her. I wished I could thrust my cock into her mouth until she gagged, and I'd taunt her until she caved and submitted to my every demand.

But I was satisfied to an extent, too. Lying there and waking up slowly, I recalled the tight, wet vise of her pussy on my dick, her sexy mewls and determined, ravenous kisses.

Tessa could be the lover I'd always dreamed of, the woman I thought I'd never find—if she could compromise and meet me in the middle like I was used to when fucking a woman.

She stirred, as though she could sense I was thinking about her.

And I want her again. Even if I couldn't take her hard like I yearned to. Even if I refused to push her and test her limits in what she could submit to.

Despite it all, I wanted her again and again, however I could, and to begin something lasting between us.

Her phone buzzed on the nightstand, and with the vibration of the device, it skittered close to the edge. I reached out to catch it before it could fall, and as I set it back on the surface, I frowned at the caller ID line.

Liam? Who the fuck is Liam? Yesterday, I'd been so on edge with how distant she was acting with me. At first, I assumed it was her reluctance to accept that I was a killer or in the Mafia, but I hadn't considered the idea that another man could be on the scene.

No. She said she was a virgin before those men caught her.

And she wouldn't have begged me to sleep with her last night and say she wanted me if she was thinking about anyone else. Right?

The jealousy that took root irked me, but before I could wake her up and ask who Liam was, her phone rang with a call, not a text this time.

Tessa stirred, programmed to the ringtone. She woke, cranky and so fucking adorable with that grouchy expression as she turned toward me and scowled at her phone in my hands.

"Goddammit." She took the device and ignored the call. "They won't stop."

"Who is it?" I asked.

She slumped back to the bed. "My parents."

Her parents whom she wanted to avoid for good.

I watched her rub her face, both her hands dragging up and down over her still sleepy expression. It was revealed as only a show of annoyance once she lowered her hands.

"I don't know what the hell I'm doing anymore, but I cannot fathom going back to them."

I took her hand and sighed as I rubbed my fingers over hers in a kneading massage. "You're here with me."

She huffed. "For now. I mean, I appreciate what you did last night, um, comforting me and all, but I know I can't stick around and bother you for good." As though she regretted speaking so candidly, she sat up more and turned worried eyes toward me. "Not that I'm expecting to or anything."

"Tess, you will stay with me for as long as you want."

She rolled her eyes. "No, I won't. You're a busy man. You've got commitments and jobs and responsibilities."

I shrugged. "I'm not too busy for you."

Her expression turned sad. "It seemed like you have been since we came here."

Fuck. Is that why she seemed distant? She thought she was a burden?

"I get it. You're a man in a high position in your, uh, organization. I don't want to interrupt and take up your time when you and Dante and Frank—"

"Franco," I corrected.

"Franco. When you guys are all gearing up to stop another Mafia family and a biker club from hurting anyone in your family again. I see that. This is a hectic time, and I don't expect you to stop and pander to me."

I growled, rolling her to her back. "I told you, Tess. I want to help you. However I can."

She sighed, rubbing her hands over my upper arms. When she didn't protest me lying over her, I hoped it was a good sign.

"I know. And I appreciate that. But I'm not going to just barge into your life. I'm complicated, and I am not holding it to you to uncomplicate anything for me."

I frowned, not liking how quick she was to shut me out after last night's way of her letting me in as deep as I could go. She couldn't only want me for sex. She was too inexperienced and naïve to be able to use sex as an escape. "How are you complicated?"

"Let's see. I've been controlled by my parents for my whole life. My dad takes all my money. My mom expects me to be some pure, good girl and do no wrong. The fact that I didn't bring my dad's car home was a huge wrongdoing, and I bet if I showed up today and told them I was raped, they wouldn't let me into their house."

I shook my head, mad that she'd be so quick to assume such a shitty future. "No. You will not be homeless, Tess."

"I don't have any money for my own place," she continued just as matter-of-factly. "I can't get my own apartment or anything, but Nina and I were trying to save up for one to share since she hated her brother mooching off her."

"That's not an issue anymore," I replied.

"Well, I guess not, with her being engaged to your dad."

I shrugged. "And the fact that Ricky is dead."

Her eyes opened wide. "Whoa. How?"

"The bikers."

She winced. "Because Nina didn't go to Reaper after that bet?"

I shrugged again. "The Devil's Brothers are ruthless."

"I can see that."

"You won't be homeless," I repeated, steering her back to explaining herself, not talking about others.

"I have no job anymore," she argued.

"I'll find you whatever position you want."

She rolled her eyes, stubborn against my arguments that she didn't have to have such a complicated life. It was her trust and faith I wanted to hear from her. Suddenly, they mattered so much more than sex—hard or soft, however it could happen. Something physical was fine, but with how quickly I'd been smitten with her, I wanted to feel something reciprocal from her.

"Then the whole thing with Elliot." She lifted her old phone and let it drop. "He's been calling too."

I frowned at the device. She had the new one, but it seemed she was still hanging on to the older one with her former number. While it might have represented a method of clinging to her past, I wondered if she debated pitching it and losing all contact with her parents.

From her perspective, it was probably scary. Without me, she'd have no one and nowhere to go—except to Elliot, who she wanted to avoid at all costs.

"I still can't believe my mom went into the account and programmed it so Nina couldn't contact me. She must have thought Nina was a bad influence." She scowled, shaking her head. "Actually, I *know* she thought Nina was a bad influence. She commented a few times about how wrong Nina was to dissuade me from marrying Elliot. She overheard us talking once, and afterward, she nagged me for having 'bad' and 'unsupportive' friends."

When we realized that Mrs. West had blocked Nina from contact, it seemed like Tessa really wasn't joking about how controlling her homelife was.

"And Elliot is a massive complication in my life."

"He doesn't have to be," I reminded her.

She peered up at me, serious and quiet for a long moment. "I'm not going to *ask* you to kill him."

I smirked at her, slightly amused. "Killing someone isn't always the simplest answer."

She blushed, looking sheepish.

"But as far as Hines is concerned, killing him would provoke more consequences than what we might want right now."

"I know."

"Nina is pregnant, and my father is obsessed with her safety. At the same time, we're preparing to eradicate the power the Giovannis and the Devil's Brothers have. It's a lot at once."

She set her hand on my arm. "All the more reason for you not to worry about me."

I stared at her, unblinking. "Too fucking late for that, Tess. I worried the second I heard you in the alley."

"But—"

I pressed my finger to her lips. "No. No *but*. I worry about you, and I will stand by my offer to help you and keep you safe. However, killing Elliot won't be feasible as we build our cases against our enemies. He's corrupt."

She nodded, grimacing at the fact.

"And he's got a long history of representing those kinds of fuckers. He was involved in criminal and civil cases that the Domino Family was dealing with. He's behind getting the bikers off scot-free from numerous charges. And we're finding evidence of embezzlement that ties him with Stefan Giovanni. While he's indirectly or directly connected to our enemies, we need to plan a proper way of getting him to forget about this supposed arrangement for you to marry him."

Tessa nodded and leaned her head against my arm.

This wasn't as intimate and peaceful as when she asked me to hold her at the other place, but I welcomed the peace to talk and be together. Through the good times and bad, I wanted her with me.

I wished all these circumstances weren't an issue, all these complications that Tessa claimed to make her a problem that I didn't have time for.

All I wanted, deep down, was a chance to take care of her in every way I could. Sexually and otherwise. Her happiness was my project, and I doubted that I'd let anything stand in my way.

"I am *not* too busy for you, Tess."

She sighed and nodded. "Okay."

Dammit. That sounded like a copout, giving me the answer I wanted to hear.

"And you are welcome to stay with me for as long as you want. You understand?"

Again, she nodded. When she threaded our fingers together, holding my hand, I exhaled and hoped that his conversation had done more good than harm.

Before we could resort to the quiet of the morning again, just sitting and being together, I asked what I'd almost forgotten about. "Who's Liam?"

She laughed lightly. "No one to be jealous of," she teased.

I smiled, realizing how hard I must have sounded when I asked that.

"An old friend, a childhood friend. I haven't seen him since he graduated from high school because he went straight into the army. We've texted and called here and there, but I've only just recently gotten a text from him. That's why I'm holding on to my old phone yet. My parents and Elliot can fuck off, but I can't lose my ties with my old buddy."

"Just friends?" I asked.

"Yes. He's like the brother I never had."

Good. The last thing I needed was to contend with competition.

"I wonder if he's going to be able to visit soon or something." She shrugged, showing how little the man mattered, almost flippant and casual about it. "And if he is…" She groaned. "I've got no clue how to make that happen."

"Hey, a friend of yours will be a friend of mine," I said calmly.

"Careful, Romeo." She squeezed my hand. "If you keep being too good to be true like this, you'll risk me falling head over heels."

I think I already have. Keeping that to myself, I lifted our joined hands and kissed her knuckle.

It's way *too soon to overwhelm her like that.* If she couldn't see herself with me and disregard details about where she'd live and not face Elliot, I wasn't sure whether she meant that as a joke or not.

14

TESSA

I thought that having sex with Romeo would reset things between us.

That was how naïve I was about men.

After the night that he woke me up with a kiss and broke me out of that nightmare, he went back to being distant and busy. I couldn't say for certain that he was going out of his way to put distance between us, but that was what it felt like.

He was attentive and caring, considerate and generous. But he acted like that in such a way that made me think I was once again a burden, a responsibility and burden among all the others that he had weighing on his shoulders.

I don't want to be an obligation. I watched him from afar, seated on a loveseat built into a bay window. He paced back and forth in the other room, talking to Franco. Or maybe it was Dante. Andy. George? I lost track, and I doubted it mattered.

All I knew for a fact was that Romeo wasn't talking to *me*.

For a week, we lasted in this waiting game. I seemed to be the only one wondering when something would happen between us. And I was left waiting because even though I sometimes felt like Romeo was watching me and always keeping tabs on me, he didn't make eye contact much. He didn't initiate anything romantic or intimate, either.

Which is probably my fault.

I'd blurted out too much of an uncensored truth, that I could fall head-over-heels for him with how well he tended to me. It was true, but also not. I was aware that having sex with him had been an excuse to avoid my past. I'd sought him out that night of the rainstorm because he was right there, warm and caring, a convenient placeholder. It was a rebound, no doubt about it.

When I considered it in that light, I hated myself a little more for *using* him. I used Romeo for sex, and that somehow cheapened it all. Of course, he'd wanted it too. He got off as well. But I disliked the notion that it only happened because of something else.

Besides, this is not the time for trying to hook up with a man. It wasn't. No matter how deeply I grew attached to Romeo and how quickly I imprinted myself on him because he'd saved me like a grand hero that night, it wasn't smart to rush into anything. Whatever Romeo and I did, it would be too close in time to the horrors I'd experienced. Until I could feel completely recovered and whole after that trauma, whatever we started—if anything—would always be tainted as *post-rape*.

Stop moping around. I sighed, restless and antsy without anything to do. This sudden freedom from my parents and my employment still felt weird. Like I *should* be doing something or else I would be lazy.

But I'd already cleaned everything. I reorganized the kitchen and scrubbed the bathroom. I wasn't sure what else I could tidy up, and reading didn't hold my interest.

If this is what the life of a kept, spoiled woman is like, I do not want to sign up. I—

Knocks sounded at the door, pulling me from my musings. Instead of looking out the window at the start of the leaves changing colors as autumn came closer, I watched Romeo walk across the room to open the door. He must have been expecting visitors because he seemed at ease and calm.

As he pulled the door wider open, Nina entered with another woman.

"Hey!" I jumped up and rushed to greet her, surprised but happy to see her. Since getting the replacement phone and learning that my mom must have manipulated something in our family account, something to prevent me from reaching out to my bestie, I chatted with Nina daily.

"I didn't know you were coming by," I told her as I furrowed my brow at the bags she handed over. Dante was super particular about her safety, and that was the reason she hadn't visited yet, but something must have changed to permit her being here now.

"Dante wanted to talk with Romeo and Franco in person." She jerked her thumb over her shoulder, indicating the front door that Romeo strode through as he disconnected his call.

"We'll be right outside," he promised before he exited.

I nodded, grateful for the security.

"So this is who's making Romeo a changed man?" the brunette asked, almost with enough snark to sound mean, yet not. Whoever she was, she sure was curious. But she was off the mark about assuming I was changing anything about him.

"Tess, this is Eva, Romeo's cousin. Eva, this is my best friend, Tessa West."

Eva looked me over, from my bare feet to the top of my blonde bob. A twist of her lips was all the judgment she gave me, but I didn't know whether I passed or failed. I lifted my hand in a small wave. "Hi."

"Yeah." Eva huffed, handing over a bag. "I'm guessing you'll like what Nina brought. Not the things in these bags."

I peered through them all, seeing that they'd brought more clothes. If not for them, I wouldn't have had anything. "Wow. Thanks, girls."

"Well, these too," Eva added as she pulled a strip of something out of the bag in my left hand. Condoms.

My cheeks heated so fast, and I laughed. "Oh, wow."

"Eva!" Nina rolled her eyes and shoved them back into the bag. "Don't pressure her."

"I'm not." Eva crossed her arms. "But I can insinuate." Something almost like a smile crossed her face, and I wondered why Romeo's getting some mattered to her.

"Well, that deed was already done," I admitted, surprisingly not shy about confessing it. Nina was my best friend, so I had no issues being so upfront around her. Eva seemed a little cool, but I didn't care.

"Already?" Nina laughed and headed toward the couch. "How? When? Why?"

Eva sat as well. "Why? Is that even a question in this context? Why else would they fuck?"

Nina firmed her lips in a scolding expression as I sat. "Well, after what Tessa just experienced, it would be surprising is all."

Eva raised her brows, and I sighed. *May as well say it.*

"Romeo came into the bedroom when I was crying from a nightmare about how I was raped. And I asked him to help me forget about it all."

Nina winced. "Uh-oh."

Eva smiled. "Well, damn."

"Huh?" I volleyed my gaze between them.

Nina cleared her throat. "It's, um, well, asking him to have sex with you so you could forget something else... It sounds like you were just asking him to perform a chore or something."

I sighed. "I know. I don't like how that sounds."

"Hey, he wouldn't have done it if he wasn't interested," Eva said.

"But he's *not*. Not anymore." I shook my head, hating to complain. "Ever since, he's aloof and busy. I want him so damn bad. Not just to further break down the memory of my trauma, but because I miss him and want to experience that closeness again."

"He's not interested?" Eva asked.

I shook my head. "No. I'm getting so frustrated about it all, but it seems like he's insisting that we only be friends."

"Have you asked, or told him, what you want?"

"No." I cringed. "I mean, I thought I sort of implied that I wanted it to happen again. Can't he just tell?"

Both women smiled and shook their heads.

Dammit. "I don't even know how to start or what to say." I shrugged and hated how weak I sounded. "I never had time to date much. I've never made a move on a guy."

"Just tell him the truth," Eva suggested.

"I want to. But aside from being nervous to speak up like that and risk rejection, I'm starting to struggle with wondering if I'm even good enough for him."

Nina smirked while Eva shrugged. I deadpanned at her immediate lack of confidence. *Jeez, thanks.*

"Or if I'm bad in bed," I added. *Since it was my first* real *time.*

Eva rolled her eyes while Nina shook her head. "No. I doubt that's it. It's not likely."

"How would you know? Or how would *I* know?"

"If you spoke up and just asked," Eva said.

I gawked at her. "I'm not asking him if I was bad in bed."

"Direct communication is always best," she preached.

I was sure that it was, but I couldn't imagine asking Romeo for confirmation like that.

"I've come to realize that Romeo is a serious sort of man who is sometimes hard to read," Nina said. "Maybe direct communication would be helpful."

"It would. Romeo's always been like that, serious and closed-off, so putting him on the spot and opening a direct line of conversation would be smart.

Nina laughed suddenly. "Oh, my God." She cracked up even more, and I wondered if the pregnancy hormones could make her loopy.

"Oh, my *God*," she repeated around her tears from laughing so hard.

"What?" I asked, glancing at Eva, who stared at Nina like she was a lunatic.

"If you hook up with Romeo and marry, then I'd be your stepmother-in-law!"

We laughed with her.

"You are both messed up," Eva teased.

"No, there won't be any marrying," I said as I finished giggling. *He's friend-zoned me already. I can't see him popping the question with that trend.* "We're just…"

"I was just teasing," Nina said, seeming concerned about potentially offending me somehow.

"I know, I know. In all seriousness, I'm just so glad and grateful that I don't have to deal with my parents anymore. Or Elliot."

Nina raised her brows. "You haven't talked to them once?"

I shook my head. "Nope. My old phone is blowing up with calls and texts from them, but I don't answer. I haven't since that night that Romeo rescued me. I made the mistake of unlocking that phone once. And I saw enough from my mom to not want to bother at all."

"What'd she say?" Nina asked.

"She accused me of being a spoiled brat for running off with some man when I should be focusing on marrying Elliot like they want."

"That's messed up," Eva said.

But also, somehow true.

From all accounts, with us living together in this isolated, remote cabin, it was all too easy to *feel* like I'd run off with him.

But not as a woman he'd want.

15

ROMEO

After I spoke with my father and Franco for a while, I asked why they wanted to meet in person.

My father shrugged. "Nina wanted to see Tessa. And I wanted to check on you."

Franco and I shared a look. My father cared about everyone in the family, but he never made a habit of personally checking up on me. I was thirty-one, not three. "How come?"

"Just with this new woman in your life…" He rocked on his heels and shrugged. "Making sure you're not too busy in La-La Land and in love and lowering your guard."

Franco grunted a laugh. "Romeo lowering his guard? Ever?"

I smiled at his backhanded praise. I was the serious guy, but I wasn't convinced that was a bad thing. "I'm fine."

"You won't deny anything I just said?" My father smirked.

"I will. I'm not in anything with Tess." I hated the sound of those words out of my mouth. I wanted to be, but I had to do this carefully and at her pace. I hadn't forgotten how she'd told me that she was *at risk* of falling for me. The wording implied that I was a risk to consider and that she shouldn't normally want someone like me. I couldn't fault her for not wanting to jump into anything too soon with both feet, but it would ease my worries if it seemed like she was nudging one foot closer to taking a leap of faith on me.

"But you want to be?" Franco guessed good-naturedly. He knew when to joke and poke fun. "Guess you're taking my advice to get laid, then. Huh?" *Or not.*

I deadpanned at him. "Tess and I are making sure she can cope with her trauma. I've promised to help her however she needs me."

Which is awfully telling because she hasn't approached me for a whole week after we had sex.

My father nodded, patting both of us on the back. "All right. I've seen enough to know you're doing fine here."

Ha. I felt halfway crazy from wanting her and even more insane with the determination to let her come to me, to give her the right of way to initiate anything more.

And if she does, I'll take whatever vanilla simplicity she can handle and deal with it.

I sighed, then nodded at them. "We'll check in more often soon." This cabin was so remote, and the surveillance at the gate would alert me to anyone coming on the path. Other than the one road toward this place, thick brush and steep slopes prevented anyone from trespassing too close. Besides, no one would be able to easily link this cabin to a Constella family member.

Franco left first, and then my father left with Nina and Eva. I ignored her teasing looks she gave me in parting, but I had to wonder what kind of girl talk those three had gotten up to while I stepped out with the others.

"I'm going to do a quick perimeter check," I told Tess.

"Okay." She nodded, looking up from where she perched on the couch with a new paperback Nina must have brought for her.

"Remember—"

"If I feel like anything is wrong, grab the gun and hide," she finished for me.

I smiled, glad she hadn't forgotten what I declared to be the first rule here. After seeing her with that dinky steak knife at the other place I hadn't finished renovating, I planned to prepare her with lessons of real defense. She admitted to not being familiar with guns, but she seemed all right with holding it and knowing how to use it in a general sense.

As soon as it's safer to move around, I'm arranging for lessons. Self-defense, too. I would spare her nothing. Tessa would learn to kick ass, even though I'd handle that for her.

Checking the perimeter was a task that needed to be done, regardless of the surveillance tech and equipment set up out here. It never made sense to cut corners, and every time I checked the perimeter, I felt better for seeing firsthand that we weren't in danger.

I needed the moment to clear my head as well. Being cooped up and in close proximity in the cabin was wearing on me. I felt like she was suffering from the same longing and desire I resisted, but until she told me how she felt, I wouldn't dare assume.

Maybe she's just shy. I furrowed my brow as I scanned the woody path, looking out for anything that seemed off at the same time that I thought about Tess. I recalled clearly how she was quiet before we had sex. And timid, like she was learning how to kiss. When she admitted that she was a virgin before those men raped her, anger streamed through me and I had to control my temper. But in telling me that, she was conveying how clueless she was.

I wonder if she would know what to say or do to initiate anything further...

A sharp blast of pain hit me in my arm, and I spun from the impact. Agonizing throbs and stings of tingling numbness radiated from the bullet hole. I was shot. I *had* lowered my guard thinking about Tess. It was as if my fucking father and cousin had jinxed me.

I turned, clapping my hand to the wound as I dropped to the ground. Behind me, I saw a sniper take off from a thick clump of brush.

You motherfucker. I got up to sprint after him, but with my head pounding and blood streaming too fast from the wound, I staggered to a stop.

No.

He was running away, prompting me to chase. The asshole ran in the opposite direction of the cabin, and I worried that it was a diversion to get me separated from Tess.

No!

I refused to let anything happen to her. When I told her and promised her that I would do anything and everything to help her and keep her safe, I meant it with every fiber of my being. I couldn't be so stupid as to fall for a ploy. If one sniper was here, then others could be lurking near as well.

Gritting my teeth to the pain, I lowered my bloody hand so I could run with both arms low to swing. I pumped my legs as hard as I could, dashing back to the cabin. Birds still sang. Leaves flittered to the forest floor. Bugs buzzed. All seemed normal and well, like this was any other ordinary day out in the vast wilderness, but it was not.

Fear charged me to go faster yet. Riding the high of the adrenaline rush, I felt less of the pain from being shot and more of the bitter panic and fury lancing through me.

I had to protect her. I had to get there in time. There were no excuses, not a single fucking one, for her getting hurt on my watch.

At last, I reached the cabin, coming up on two men trying to bust in a window. One raised a club-like stick, and the other looked around, scanning for any threats. Through the window, I made out the shape of Tess holding the gun up at the window as she backed away. With frightened eyes, she noticed me past the two men at the window.

They must have noticed her looking at something behind them, because the one with the stick nudged at the guy on lookout. In unison, they turned their heads and sought me out.

My chest rose and fell so fast, heaving for air as I tried to catch my breath. Already, I was getting dizzy and lightheaded from losing so much blood. My T-shirt was damp from warm blood, and I felt the numbness spread along my arm.

Before these fuckers could break the window or try anything with me, I narrowed my eyes and lifted my non-dominant hand. I'd trained with both, just for shitty situations and circumstances like this.

Aiming my gun precisely, I shot one dead between the eyes. He dropped back against the window, and as he dropped, blood smeared on the surface.

"Fuck," the other said. He lurched to the side to run for cover, but two more shots from my gun removed any function his knees might have once had. Crying out and cursing, he pounded his fist to the ground as he strained to roll over.

"What the fuck do you think you're doing?" I demanded as I stalked closer. He'd beat me to bleeding out, but I clamped my hand on my wound as I kicked his gun away.

His neck flexed as he clenched his teeth, scrambling over the leaves and grass. He didn't get far because I stood on his nuts.

"A Giovanni?" I snarled, guessing that this pair had to be men from Stefan Giovanni's organization. They weren't too familiar, but they were dressed too sharp to be members of the Devil's Brothers MC.

"Fuck you, Constella."

I risked the agony of not compressing my wound to step back, shoot his nuts, then stand on the site again. His screams would scare Tessa, but I had to go this far. I had to be this macabre to get the answers I needed.

"What the fuck are you doing here?" I gritted my teeth at the pain locking over my shoulder, and I pressed my foot down harder. "Talk. Now!"

"Stefan is pissed that Dante wouldn't support him with the gun routes." He growled, trying to tough out the hits. "And he wants to attack him however he can."

"By taking me out?"

He nodded, shakily and quickly. "Yes. Since Dante refused to align the Constellas with the Giovannis, Stefan wants to take them out. All of you."

I shook my head. That stupid fucker. I'd never really cared for Stefan. If he was the selfish idiot that he was today back when he was younger, I couldn't understand why my father was ever his friend. Stefan was nothing like my father. "I thought Stefan was aligning with the fucking bikers." I knew he was because we'd recently had to save Nina from being taken by the collaborating groups.

The man nodded, gasping for air through the agony he had to be feeling. Kneecaps shattered, balls and dick blasted to pulp, yeah, he wouldn't be feeling too great.

"He is aligning with the MC," he replied, "because he likes to always keep his options open."

In other words, two-time the whole goddamn world if he could get away with it.

"How'd you find me here?" I pressed harder on my wound.

"Followed… Franco," he replied, squeezing his eyes shut tight. "We know he's been setting up spies to watch us, and we've had our men tailing him."

And he and my father had decided to check in on me, leading the enemy closer.

"Dante's got his place too heavily guarded." The man was singing like a canary, telling all now. "He travels like that too, guards and security."

Of course, he does. He's protecting Nina now, and their baby. I thought I was over the top in wanting to keep Tess safe, but I wondered if I should follow my father's lead. Keep the women under layers of security—not rely on hiding and staying remote.

"Once we saw Franco heading in the same direction as Dante, we knew this would be a good chance to take someone out."

"What about the other time? At my other place?" I demanded.

"The rundown house?" He shook his head. "Stefan said Reaper volunteered to strike there."

"And now you'll all strike out." I lifted my gun and shot him between his eyes. It was a mercy kill, but also an act of impatience. I was bleeding a lot. I didn't have time to interrogate him like this. Getting to Tessa and reassuring her that she was safe was also an important goal.

That does it. We're moving again. I'll move her as many times as I need to in order to keep her safe and unharmed.

I staggered toward the door, breathing hard and wincing with every step. The impact of my footsteps juddered through me, and I blinked away the blackness creeping in from the edge of my vision.

"Tess." I cleared my throat and tried to call out for her louder before I slumped onto the door. "Tess, it's me."

I lost the fight with gravity. Weak and breathing hard with the dizzying blood loss, I fell and aimed to break my drop with the door.

She opened it right then, though, and I plummeted forward. I crashed onto the hardwood floor, halfway inside with my body on the threshold.

"Romeo!"

I whooshed out a deep breath, glad to hear her sweet voice.

We need to move. This place is compromised. I have to hide you better. All those valid thoughts remained just that, unspoken and trapped in my mind. I couldn't speak. I could barely move as the darkness crept closer and quicker.

"Romeo!" She screamed it as she dropped to her knees and laid her hands on me.

Then I was out. Right when I had to stay up and alert to save *her* from anyone coming back and making good on this vendetta Stefan was determined to see through, no matter the costs.

16

TESSA

"Romeo!" He slumped to the floor as soon as I wrenched the door open. Without putting his arms out or turning to break into the drop, his body plummeted like a lifeless sack.

"Fuck. *Romeo*!" I sank to my knees, ignoring the ache of pressing my still-healing wounds to the hard surface. My heart hammered so fast, I felt like I was on the verge of passing out, but that was the very last thing we needed. What good could I be if I was lying on the floor next to him, out of it and unable to achieve any sense of safety?

"Romeo. Please. Romeo, wake up." I grabbed his arm and tried to roll him over. His right arm and side were soaked in blood, so I didn't touch him there. But tugging on his left got him to budge a bit. He was big, so heavy even when unconscious, but I strained and pulled until I maneuvered him right side up.

His face was slack and his eyes remained closed. As I grabbed something out of the bags of clothes on the floor, I shook it out for makeshift compression. Nina and Eva likely dropped them off for me to wear, but it was the closest thing at hand to push down on the bloody holes on Romeo's upper arm.

"Romeo. Wake up."

Fear gripped me tight as I tried to compress the bleeding. I'd been rooted in terror—*again*—with today's episode of hell. When I spotted those two men out the window, about to smash it in, I grabbed the gun, just like Romeo had instructed me to in case trouble came near. I was so skittish that I got the gun out when he left. That was how nervous I was. And it was a good thing that I had.

Those two men showing up scared me, but I had the foresight to get the gun and back up to safety.

Seeing Romeo shoot one was the moment I swore my heart skipped a beat. It palpitated under the stress, but when he shot at the other one and made him scream, I lost the willpower to watch. Hiding behind the couch wasn't a tall or thick enough wall to block out what was happening. But I stayed there, wishing the gruesome memories away until I heard Romeo call out for me.

"Please, Romeo. Wake up."

In another rush of being tense and fueled with adrenaline alone, I stared at his face and chest, making sure that he *was* breathing. He was out cold but capable of respiration. That had to be a good thing, but I could *not* handle this on my own.

Danicia? She was the first person I thought to call, but I didn't want to risk scooting away from Romeo long enough to grab my phone.

"Romeo. Please, please wake up." I blinked at the burn of tears stinging my eyes. Sniffling, I refused to cave to all these emotions swirling within me. I couldn't be sad or scared. I had to remain strong for him, logical and quick to action. Yet, as I tried to find my phone while pressing the shirt to his wounds, I struggled with the terrible worry that replayed like a pesky news ticker in my mind.

What if he dies? What if he doesn't wake up? What if he dies!

The buzz of his phone made me flinch. It came from him, vibrating through him, and I removed one bloody hand to grab it out from his pocket.

The caller ID showed Franco's name, and I answered immediately.

"Franco!"

"Wait. What? Tessa?"

"Help! Come back to the cabin."

Squealing sounds came from his end. "Why? What happened? Tell me what happened."

"Romeo was shot. A couple of men tried to break in and he was shot. He shot one. Both. But they were all shot and—"

"Is anyone still there?" The roar of an engine filled his end, and I hoped that meant he was speeding back here. They hadn't left that long ago, but I bet my sense of time was all out of whack, skewed by fear. "Are you safe?"

"They're dead."

"Who's dead?" he demanded.

Romeo had yet to flinch. I winced as I leaned on his wounds and prayed he wouldn't join those other two men. "The men. Romeo was shot, but he's still breathing."

"I'm on my way. Stay put."

I nodded, even though he couldn't see. "He's lost a lot of blood." My voice cracked on the end of that reply, but I cleared my throat, determined to stay as strong and calm as possible. Those men were dead. Franco was rushing to help. As soon as we could get Romeo to the hospital, things had to turn around.

"I'm on my way. Keep your eyes open, Tessa, and look out."

I nodded again, then let the phone slide down from where I'd tucked it between my shoulder and cheek.

"Please, Romeo. Please, don't die." I swallowed hard, my throat thick again as I feared the worst. I couldn't take my eyes off him, staring at his chest and knowing it was moving. I felt the thump of his heart beat with my pinky pressed on his torso.

"You can't die," I begged quietly, knowing how irrational and hysterical I sounded despite the quietness of my voice. I'd scream it if I had the energy, but at the moment, I was putting all my energy and effort into stemming his blood loss and watching for his respiration.

Franco ordered me to look out, but I couldn't. Not well, at least. With Romeo's body halfway out the door, I'd have to drag him inside to secure us inside and know that we were safe. Staying put seemed vulnerable, but also not. I had a clear view of the front yard, and as such, I saw the approach of an SUV from a distance as it climbed the slope up to the cabin.

"He's coming. Help is coming," I told Romeo, doubting he could hear me. It didn't matter whether he could or not. I partly said it to reassure myself.

I suddenly felt so damn stupid. Just an hour ago, my worries had circled around the confusion of why he didn't seem to want me anymore. The anxiety of realizing that if I wanted Romeo to know that I was interested in him, I would have to speak up and communicate that with him, something I'd never been bold enough to do before with anyone else in my life.

I had so much to tell him and express to him. All the gratitude I felt from him saving me. Every bit of adoration and curiosity he'd instilled in me by having sex when I asked for help with my demons. And each moment of respect and patience. I wanted him to know how he'd changed my life, and I *had* to have a chance to tell him. It would be too cruel not to.

"Don't you dare die on me," I said as the SUV slammed to a stop. "We've only just started, Romeo, and I can't imagine you gone."

A single tear slipped free, but I sniffled and looked up as Franco ran close.

"I'm trying to compress the blood," I said as he dashed toward the cabin. In his hand was his gun, and as he neared us, he scanned the scene.

"Good. Good." He lowered, quickly assessing Romeo. As he lowered to the floor, he handed me his gun. "Hold this and keep a lookout."

I lifted one blood-coated hand to take it. Even though my fingers were shaky, I gripped the firearm. He stooped down to pick up Romeo, and I had no choice but to scoot back and stand out of the way. Giving Franco the clearance to hoist Romeo up, I winced and spotted him, extending my free hand toward him.

"He passed out and fell flat on his face," I added.

"Okay." He strained, tightening his facial features as he pulled off a squat-like lift. Romeo was in his arms, and he didn't delay. "Go out and open the door to the back."

I did, looking around for anyone else sneaking up close. I stood outside, still scanning the cabin and the forest as Franco put Romeo into the backseat. He only got him in part of the way.

"Go around the other side and pull him in. I need you to stay back there and compress the wound."

I nodded as he took his gun back. We were both covered in red, grisly and stinking of the metallic scent of all that blood this hero of a man had lost. But I didn't need to be told twice. Franco covered for me, the lookout, as I ran around the SUV and climbed inside.

He shut the door after me and ran back to the cabin, hauling the door shut so it'd lock. In the backseat, I put my arms under Romeo's armpits and tugged him further into the vehicle.

Franco took off his jacket and tossed it to me. "Good. Now press on that bleeding."

I applied the pressure again, watching for Romeo's chest to continue to rise and fall. It did, and Franco slammed the door shut before getting in the driver's seat.

"Tell me exactly what happened," he said as he sped down the slope.

I repeated all that I could remember, careful not to leave out any detail of what happened after he and Dante left with Nina and Eva. Franco was patient, narrowing his eyes as he glanced into the rearview mirror to check on me and Romeo.

Before long, we reached a hospital. He pulled up to the ER entrance, and I scrambled out of the car with the medics and techs helping to get Romeo out.

"Are you wounded?" one triage nurse asked me as Romeo was placed on a gurney.

"No." I shoved past her, adamant to stay with him. I couldn't be parted from him. Not now. Maybe not ever. "I have to stay with him."

"Only one family member is allowed—"

"He's my fiancé," I scolded. It was a lie, but no guilt came with saying it. I would do anything to stay with Romeo. My fear was scaled too high, this trepidation that if I lost sight of him now, I'd never see him again.

This was no mild case of lust that pulled me to him. It wasn't only physical desire that I craved with this man. My feelings had grown so quickly, and I would no longer deny how much I cared for Romeo.

It wasn't the need for intimacy in bed, nor was this another expression of my gratitude for his saving me.

It was love. My heart wouldn't go on if I was taken from him too soon.

Fortunately, the nurse and techs realized that I wouldn't take no for an answer.

"All right. This way."

With a streamline of commotion and haste, Romeo was wheeled inside. I rushed to keep up with them, but I caught sight of Franco lingering back by his car, his phone to his ear. He noticed me and waved, indicating for me to stick with Romeo.

And that was just what I did. I ran alongside the gurney, following the crew inside and praying that they wouldn't be too late to save him and wake him up.

He had to wake up.

He just had to, and as soon as he did, I had an awful lot of honest words to share with him.

I ran, watching his face as the medical techs began to take over and tell each other what to do.

Please, Romeo. I think I might already love you. And I can't lose you.

17

ROMEO

I woke up and found my father scrolling on his phone. He wore a loopy, smug smile, and I rolled my eyes at the fact that he was likely checking out a naughty text from Nina while I lay here suffering.

Actually... I tensed my back and felt less pain shooting down my arm. *It's not that bad.*

For the whole night, I was in and out of consciousness. They must have given me something basic for a sedation because I wasn't overly groggy and nauseated from having surgery.

"I'm bleeding to death and you're sexting your fiancée?" I joked as I lifted my free hand to rub my face.

He cleared his throat, putting his phone down as he faced me. "How are you feeling?"

"Like I'm no longer bleeding to death."

He nodded. "They stitched you up quickly. You passed out from the blood loss, but they determined you didn't need a transfusion."

That was good news. Maybe that meant I would be out of here sooner than later. I hated to be idle, and with the threat of what landed me in here, I was determined to stay active in protecting my family.

And Tess.

"Where's Tess?" Now that I was awake, someone had to clue me in. The last person I recalled wanting to see, the last one I'd been with, was her.

"She just stepped outside in the hallway." He stood, arching his back and smiling down at me. "You gave her a scare, but she's not as weak as she looks."

I furrowed my brow. *Who's saying that she looks weak?*

"She's been in here the entire time." His lips quirked up into a twist. "She told them that she was your fiancée to be allowed to stay at your side."

I raised my brows. I had to have fallen when I passed out, but I didn't remember hitting my head.

"She confided in me and Franco that it was a lie. Something she said just to stay with you."

I nodded. "If I proposed, you'd know."

"Would I?" He clasped his hands in front of him and peered at me. "You've been alone with her and getting close."

"Not to the point of making her mine," I argued. *But I would if I knew she'd accept me.*

He shrugged, feigning indifference but appearing amused. "It would be a kicker, though. If *you* rushed into a relationship even faster than I did with Nina."

I rolled my eyes. "Funny."

"What's not funny is what she told us while you were in surgery."

"Stefan sent two men to the cabin." *Wait. The sniper.* "Three."

He nodded, graver now with no sign of a smile on his lips or laughter in his eyes. "Franco had men sweep the area. They found the sniper who hit you. He tripped and busted his ankle, so they didn't have a hard time locating him."

"And the two I killed near the cabin?"

"Disposed of." He didn't need to ask me to justify the injuries or explain a thing. He got it.

"I kept one alive for information."

He crossed his arms. "I'm listening."

"Stefan is furious that you wouldn't align with him or back him up with the gun routes." This wouldn't be a surprise. We all knew this. "He sent the Devil's Brothers men to the other house I was at with the plan of taking me out to attack you."

He shook his head. A murderous scowl remained on his face.

"He had his men come out to the cabin to try again."

"That motherfucker," he groused.

"He also said that Stefan was frustrated with the inability to attack you directly. Since Nina's there and is expecting, you've ramped up the security forces to the point he has no way to get in."

Smiling smugly, he nodded once. "That's correct. And I don't let her leave the house without ample security."

"Which is what I need to arrange for Tessa," I said as I sat up more, pleased that the motion didn't put me in excruciating pain. "I can't rely on being remote and using that as a level of safety. The fucking storm disabled the wires for the surveillance cameras at the road."

"It's all outdated," he said, annoyed. "You should just bring Tessa to the house. Nina would love having her close."

And then she wouldn't even need me *for friendship.* I felt selfish to want to keep Tessa to myself, but until we could address this tension between us and figure out how to be together, I didn't want any obstacles to stand in the way. Nina wasn't an obstacle, but she'd be a distraction.

"No. But I intend to move her somewhere closer in the city."

"Whatever you decide," he said, letting me call the shots where Tessa was concerned.

We didn't speak any further.

The door opened, and my heart rate kicked up with the excitement that it could be Tessa walking in, but it wasn't. Instead, a doctor came in with a nurse. My father remained standing and out of the way as the doctor spoke with me. The nurse checked my vitals—all satisfactory—and I was glad for how fortunate I was with this incident.

"It looks like you're on track to be discharged tomorrow—"

"Why not today?" my father asked, cutting off the doctor.

"I would recommend at least one night of monitoring, given his blood loss."

I shook my head, glancing between the nurse and the doctor. "My vitals are looking good, right? I don't want to stay any longer than necessary."

"We have medical staff members available at home," my father added.

Danicia would certainly be a help—if I needed her. This wasn't my first rodeo. I'd been shot and stitched up before. I counted on a recovery period, and I would do the exercises and stretches required to be whole again.

"I don't recommend…" The doctor pursed his lips at my father's stern look. "I can arrange for the paperwork to be started shortly."

"*Now*," my father advised.

The doctor nodded, but the nurse rolled her eyes as she draped her stethoscope around her neck.

After they walked out, Franco entered. "Ready to go?" He grinned, looking from me to my father. "I'm guessing from the way the doc and nurse were smirking that you told them you wanted the express ticket outta here."

"Correct," I said as I swung my legs over the edge of the bed. Wincing and testing my range of motion, I sat up and stretched the best I could. Perhaps leaving wasn't what the doctor preferred, but it wasn't like I was a usual patient. I had security issues to deal with. A woman to check out.

Tess had to have been so scared, seeing me kill a man. I hoped she hadn't been within view of my shooting up and torturing that second man. While she was aware that I was a killer, I didn't want to demonstrate it in real time.

"She compressed your wounds as soon as you passed out on her," Franco said when I asked what happened to bring me to the hospital. My father assisted me in getting dressed and clearing out the room, and I was humbled with how weak and fragile the human body could be when it was pushed too far and shot.

"I happened to call you, and she answered, telling me that you needed help."

Good girl, Tess. Good girl. But I already knew she was made of stronger stuff. She wasn't a woman prone to hysterics and freaking out without acting on a threat.

"We brought you here, and she stayed the whole time, no matter how much any of us tried to talk her into going and cleaning up."

I frowned, glancing at the window. "How long have I been here?"

"Hmm, last night and into the morning," Franco said. "They sewed you up last night but let your body rest."

Hazy memories were there. I recalled coming awake after the surgery, but nothing past it.

"Here you go," the nurse said as she returned. Her tone was flippant and sassy as she handed my discharge papers to my father.

He didn't bat a lid at her attitude. He simply took the papers and tucked them into the inner pocket of his jacket.

Danicia would make sure I followed the instructions to the final detail.

"A little through and through won't keep a Constella down, huh?" Franco joked as he held the door open for me.

"Not at all," I replied as I exited the room.

We came to a stop as I spotted Tessa. Just seeing her blonde head and her slim body soothed an anxious part of my soul. She'd become such an important feature in my life. Knowing she was near calmed me.

But she wasn't feeling the same. Facing off with an older woman, she set her hands on her hips and shouted back.

I didn't know what the hell they were arguing about in the hallway of a hospital, but I strode toward her, more than ready to stand up for her in whatever this situation was.

18

TESSA

"I've never been more disappointed in you!" my mother shouted.

She was usually a quiet woman, preferring to not make waves in order to do the least amount of work possible. Her existence was one of complaints and misery as she wished for a different life of luxury that she'd never obtain on her low income.

"Running off like that! How dare you?"

"Oh." I huffed and crossed my arms. "I imagine it's been torture."

She fumed, baring her teeth at the audacity I had to sass back. "It has, you ungrateful, spoiled, selfish, and good-for-nothing little bit—"

"Excuse me?" Romeo strode forward, cutting between us. His bandaged arm was still supported in a sling, wrapped with numerous bandages.

I smiled at him, so glad that he was awake and moving so well. The doctors had told us that he'd recover well, that the through-and-through wound bled a lot but missed main blood vessels and bones.

His muscles would need support to rebuild, but his prognosis was very optimistic.

I intended to help him through it every step of the way. I'd never be able to repay him for all I'd done, but I wanted to try.

Gazing at him with lovestruck eyes, I sighed and took in how strong and healthy he looked after being shot and bleeding out like that. After the fear of losing him, I was overjoyed to see him hale and hearty.

"Don't speak to her like that," he said, looking my mother up and down.

She bristled, not liking anyone to interfere when she was belittling me. Not even my dad could get a word in when she was on a roll. He just had to take his turn and yell at me after she was done.

Running into her here was inevitable. She was an LPN at this very hospital, and my luck ran out when I left Romeo's room to let Dante have a few moments with his son.

"And who are *you* to tell me what to do?" she sassed back, clueless as to who he was.

I considered him from what she saw. The dark circles under his eyes from a long night of poor sleep. The redness on his cheek from falling to the floor. His clothes were clean and not bloody, at least. Franco brought a change of clothes for both of us since our clothing was so red.

Romeo looked tired and disheveled. Still handsome as ever, according to me, but tired and worn down.

She pushed past him to face me directly, oblivious of his lethal stare that he didn't take off her for a single second.

"I've got every right to tell this brat how disappointed I am in her. Running off, quitting her job, stealing my husband's car—"

Oh! I stepped closer and got in her face. "I didn't steal anything!"

"You didn't bring his car home after work. That's the same thing as stealing."

"I didn't bring his car home—" I stuttered and stopped short. Words failed to form, and I closed my mouth. A glance at Romeo showed that he'd lightened up his glare at my mom to frown at me, knowing exactly what happened that night.

I hadn't stolen my dad's car because I'd left it right where it was parked while I worked. And I hadn't driven that car anywhere because I'd been reduced to a numb mess after being raped.

I couldn't air that fact here. Telling my mom about what happened was something I didn't want to ever share with her because in a backward, twisted way, she'd try to convince me that it was somehow my fault, that I wasn't a victim but an idiot who'd encouraged those men to chase after me.

She gathered steam while I faltered. "You didn't bring his car home. He had to go get it and be late—"

"For a fucking fishing store?" I growled. "Tough shit."

She lifted her hand to slap me but at the last second, noticed how much attention she was getting, arguing with me in a public place like this.

"You don't come home. You don't pay up—"

"Pay up for *what?*" a woman snapped.

My mom turned as Eva strode forward. Compared to my mom in her scrubs and dumpy, dated hairstyle, Romeo's cousin looked like a princess, royal and gorgeous. Maybe she was high-maintenance with her perfect makeup, immaculate designer clothes, and flawless skin and hair, but that was her choice. And she rocked it.

"I asked you a question. Pay for *what?*" Eva demanded.

"It's none of your business. This is between me and my daughter."

"Your daughter? Or your free labor?"

My mom gaped at her, stunned and furious. "What the fuck? How *dare* you speak to me like that."

"It's true," I retorted. "It's true. You and Dad treat me like free labor, making me pay rent to live with you since the day I turned sixteen. You never gave me a chance to save up to move out because you mooched off me and guilted me into giving you my money, all because Dad never wanted to work a day in his life."

She lifted her hand to slap me again. I'd pushed her too far, throwing these truths in her face.

Romeo was quicker. Before she could lay a hand on me, he grabbed her wrist and stopped her midair. "Do. Not. Touch. Her."

She wrestled and fought his grip. Wrenching her arm away, she stepped further from him and scowled. "Oh, so this is what you thought to do? Run off with a man like him?" Again, she dragged her judgmental glare up and down him, disdain clear in her eyes and wrath evident in her sneer.

"Answer me," she demanded. "You thought you could run off with a man like this?"

I couldn't stand the thought of her criticizing Romeo. He had no faults she could count. He had no flaws that could make him a horrible person. Not to me. "I didn't run," I said, hating that I was trying to deescalate the situation by focusing on my actions.

"It looks like you did." She lowered her furious gaze to my hand that Romeo took. As if he felt the ire of her attention, he squeezed my fingers with a comforting pressure. To ground me, to remind me that I had him for support. The man just got out of surgery, and here he was, taking on my mother for me.

"It looks like you thought you could run off and follow along with a man like this one." She narrowed her eyes at him, noticing the Constella men around us. "He's a bad man, Tessa. This man isn't right for you. I know it. I can tell just by looking at him. Him and his thugs. These criminals and lowlifes."

"All right. That's enough. We done here?" Franco drawled, losing his patience as he beckoned for the Constella soldiers to help us clear out in this hallway.

"No. Nothing is done here," my mom snapped at him. She turned to me, reaching for my hand, but I smacked it away.

"Don't touch me."

"You're throwing your life away. This is a mistake. Can't you see? Running off with a stupid criminal? Look at him. He's not a good man. Elliot is."

I looked at the ceiling, so exasperated that I had zero patience for this.

"He's a good, honest man," she ranted.

"Yeah, right," Romeo quipped.

"And you need to pay attention to building your relationship with him, Tessa. Elliot is your future. Not this bad man, these thugs who avoid the law." She cringed, looking at Romeo, and made another grab for my hand.

"No." I shoved her by the shoulder, glad when she staggered back. "I'm done with you and Dad."

Romeo held my hand every step of the way as he led me down the hall, but my mom didn't give up. She just had to have the last word.

"I'm telling your father that I saw you."

I huffed. "I don't give a fuck." Seeing her was hard. Putting up with her enraged lecture was trickier yet. But with Romeo, even Eva at my side since she'd come to visit with Dante, who'd already left, I was stronger. I had my reasons to stand tall and not back down from my mom's hatred and judgment. And to hear her tell me to go back to Elliot? I was steaming and fuming inside, bottling up all this wrath until I could let it out privately.

"This is wrong, Tessa. Wrong! After all we've done for you, you think you can just quit and walk away? That's not how life works. Not like this." She hurried after us, blocked by the Constella men who followed me and Romeo.

"You are a horrible waste of life if this is what you choose. Going with an awful man like him. He's nothing but a thug! The kind of criminals Elliot helps to punish."

"Can't we walk faster?" I asked Romeo.

He frowned at me, then lifted his hand. Snapping his fingers and pointing, he gave a signal to the soldiers behind us.

They turned, reforming their positions as a group. Two men continued to exit with us, but others pivoted to prevent my mom from following us any further.

"You're nothing, Tessa. You are not my daughter if you run off with that man! You hear me?"

I winced, grateful for Romeo's comforting grip on my hand.

"Don't even think about trying to come back home. Never. Don't you dare plan on returning to us and thinking you have a place in our lives."

I gritted my teeth at her fading shouts as the Constella soldiers kept her back. "The only place I had in your lives was to bring you as much money as possible."

"Not anymore." Romeo sighed as we reached the elevator. "You don't need to worry about keeping a place in their lives at all."

I nodded, hoping that could really be true forever.

Seeing Romeo in action and on the cusp of dying—or at least it seemed like that to me when he passed out and bled so fast—put things in perspective.

I'd latched on to him as a stepping stone away from the life I knew, but if I were to lose him, not only would my heart be shattered, but I'd also have no one else in my corner. No place else to go.

I hated feeling this untethered, like anything could strike out and pound me down into hopelessness and despair. For too long, I'd been waiting on something good to land in my path, something I could rely on for more than just a dream to entertain myself or a false illusion of security.

As we rode the elevator, Franco and the soldiers in the car with us, as well as a tired-looking tech in messy scrubs, I couldn't look up. I felt Romeo's gaze on me, and it tempted me to make eye contact in the mirrored walls of the elevator car, but I just couldn't.

I felt so ashamed, so little and down, to face him. Only when we were in the backseat of a car did I turn to Romeo. Franco drove, but I was grateful for the privacy partition.

"I…"

"What?" He took my hand and kissed my knuckles.

I laughed, broken and humiliated. *I don't know what to do, where to go.* "I'm sorry she said those things about you."

His grunt of a laugh intrigued me, and I lifted my gaze to his. "What?"

He gazed at me, calmer but so serious. Like he'd tell his capo to turn this car around so he could teach my mother a lesson about making me feel worthless and stupid like this.

"I'm sorry she said you're a bad man."

Now he smiled, lighting up my world in a sick and silly way. "Tess. I *am* a bad man."

"But she's wrong. You're also a good man, Romeo." I hoped he heard the sincerity I couldn't hide.

"You saw me," he said, softly yet somberly. "You saw me kill that man."

I swallowed, feeling nervous at having to talk about this. I already knew that he was a killer. He told me that he'd avenged me and killed my rapists. But seeing it was believing it, too.

"I did." I steadied my breath, doing my best not to show any unease and prove to him that I wasn't turned off or away from him. "And I know you killed that other man."

"I tortured him," he corrected. "I couldn't kill him until I got answers from him, and I did. I need you to understand that."

I rubbed my fingers over his knuckles, needing to move somehow. "I know, and I also respect that in some areas of life, like in your family, it comes down to the concept of *kill or be killed*."

He nodded, almost seeming proud of my assessment. Then he put me on the spot. "Why do you insist on wanting to be with me, to be near me, when you know what I'm capable of?"

"Because I can't imagine being anywhere else than with you."

Because I know that I'm safest with you.

Because I get the impression that I calm you down and level out that darkness you can't escape.

"Because I care." I swallowed, my words failing me as I laid my soul bare for him. "Because I care about you, *a lot*, Romeo. And I don't want to consider being separated from you."

Not now. And not ever again.

He gazed at me for a long moment, seeming to search my face and find a reason I might hold him in such high esteem. Finally, he sighed and relaxed into his seat, prompting me to lean against him. "Then you will stay with me," he stated, simple and matter of fact as he pushed a button to lower the partition. "Franco," he said once the divider lowered. "Take us to my penthouse in the South End."

Penthouse? He had so many places to stay while I had… none. Except this moment, with him, and I clung to it as I closed my eyes and let the ride lull me to doze off.

19

ROMEO

Tessa and I moved to the penthouse that I seldom stayed in. I liked the freedom of staying wherever I pleased, unsettled and without any obligations to remain in any one location for long.

With Tessa, though, I wanted to provide her with security and stability. After her mother's hateful words of disowning her and casting her out of her house, I was driven to make sure the sweet woman belonged with me. She'd never need to test out the theory that her mom and dad wouldn't welcome her back home.

"Like this?" she asked one evening when I brought her to a shooting range. It was near the mansion my father lived in with Nina, but according to him, they wanted a quiet night in. All their nights were in, but I wouldn't push for a chance to visit. Besides, Nina and Tessa had video calls almost daily.

Tonight was another exercise in teaching her self-defense, and that included training her how to hold and use a gun. Safety was paramount. I offered Nina self-defense lessons as well, but I was certain my father would handle those.

"Higher," I coached. Standing behind her, I wrapped my arms around her and corrected her grip on the gun. Her ear protection muffs remained hanging over her neck, and the hard plastic shells knocked into mine around my neck as I stepped into her space.

Her breath hitched, and I refrained from growling. Desire coiled within me, always at a constant low burn. Pressing up against her back like this and hugging her to demonstrate a proper grip was nothing short of torture.

Fuck me. Hearing her gasps and sensing her reaction to my proximity was like playing with fire. Every little thing she did somehow became more sensual. More erotic.

I'd stopped eating with her because staring at her licking a spoon or fork was tormenting. I couldn't stay in the same room with her when she read because any time she sighed like she was reading something sentimental alerted me to watching *all* of her facial expressions. Likewise for when something urged her to huff lightly, making me curious what had annoyed or amused her.

We'd fallen in a more domesticated routine of being roommates, but with a serious tension that neither of us would talk about. I was living with her but forcing myself to keep things as platonic as possible.

Until she made a move, I had to keep my wits about me.

"Like this?" she asked, her voice breathy and low, suggesting that she struggled with her ass against my groin, my arms brushing over the sides of her breasts.

Ever so slightly, she turned her head toward mine. Her smooth cheek rubbed along mine, and I damn near shook with need.

All it would take was one inch of a pivot, a single shift to the side to bring my mouth to hers and steal a kiss. A kiss I'd been thinking about and dreaming about daily and nightly.

This woman was on my mind constantly, and I wasn't sure which of us might snap first.

"Yes." I stepped back, unable to handle the temptation of her in my arms and leaning back toward me like she wordlessly had to tell me that she needed me near.

The next night, I supervised her learning how to get out of a chokehold. The Constella soldier who sparred with her and gave her the basics of self-defense was an older man, a good guy who wouldn't cop a feel. Watching from the sides of the private gym I had here, I sighed and wondered how I might get *my* hands on her. Not to fight, but—

"How's she been doing?" Danicia asked. She'd come by to check on my arm, and I was glad that she approved of my progress so far. My gunshot wound was the reason I wasn't the one training Tessa on the mats over there. But even if I did have all of my normal range of motion, I wasn't sure if I'd be able to control my desire. Holding her. Tugging her close. Overpowering her and dropping her to the mat. It was all for an educational purpose, but with her…

"Good," I answered quickly.

Danicia laughed. "Good?"

I nodded. "Yeah."

"No more hints of trauma she's struggling to cope with?" She looked at her smart watch. "It's only been three weeks since that night. Sometimes, that kind of recovery takes months. Years."

I shrugged the shoulder of the arm that wasn't shot. "I haven't heard her crying in the middle of the night anymore."

Danicia raised her brows. "How?"

I frowned, not wanting to discuss anything too personal. I had yet to share a bed with Tess again, but that wasn't any of Danicia's business. "She leaves her door cracked open, and I leave mine cracked open as well. I'd hear her."

The former doctor crossed her arms. "And if she was, what would you do?"

Memories of the one night of vanilla sex filled me with both elation and dread. I enjoyed having Tess in the deepest way possible, but I also wanted to cringe at how mild it was. I wanted her again. I had since that night, but I grew despondent in realizing I'd never be able to ask her for what *I* wanted.

If the woman couldn't find the courage to tell me what she wanted or what she felt about me, then how could I ever expect her to be favorable to anything kinky at all?

"I would comfort her however she wanted me to," I replied, watching her with the man on the mat again. She nodded at his instructions, determined to be a good student and do as expected.

She *was* still getting over her trauma. I had to keep that forefront in my mind because it wasn't right for me to lust after her and wish for more, to be greedy with the person I wanted to take utmost care of.

"I won't push her," I added, glancing at Danicia and catching her studying me.

"You like her," she surmised, smiling sloppily.

I deadpanned.

"You have to if you want to keep her close like this." She grinned and patted my back. "Like you'd be lost without her in your life."

I exhaled a deep whoosh of air, taking a risk to be open and honest. "I *would* be lost without her. I don't know how she got under my skin so quickly, but she has."

"Does she know?"

I frowned. "I don't know how she can't." I made love with her, letting her take charge of it all. I held her hand when she looked unsure. I provided all her necessities, making a mental list of her little quirks and preferences for what she seemed to like to eat, drink, and wear.

"Well, with her limited experience, always busy working and never actually dating a man, maybe she needs you to be direct and explain it all. Less miscommunication and all."

I had to be direct and explain that I wanted to pound into her tight pussy without mercy? *Yeah, right. Not happening.*

"Something is happening between us," I admitted, "but it's complicated. She's naïve and innocent. Inexperienced. And I've made it my mission to see to her safety and happiness."

"But what if her happiness includes this 'something' that's brewing between you?"

I sighed, wishing I knew how to better word it. "She wants to be close to me. I can tell. But it might not be the same as what I feel for her."

"Because I care about you, a lot, Romeo. And I don't want to consider being separated from you."

I'd replayed Tessa's words in my mind over and over on repeat. It sounded promising, but her affection was likely gratitude, not true interest.

"She cares," Danicia guessed, nodding like she was an expert at reading people.

"She told me that she cares about me. But she might have said that only for the sake of expressing a form of hero worship."

Danicia smirked at me.

"If we'd met in any other circumstances, I don't know if she'd feel the same."

The tall woman smiled smugly, like she knew something I didn't. "Then maybe it's time to ask. And find out."

I rolled my eyes, turning away to walk out of the gym. I'd had enough of this introspective bullshit. It was hard enough to be in my head all the time, obsessing about Tess and feeling confused on how to make things smoother between us.

I didn't need to borrow Danicia for any shrink time. Besides, I hadn't revealed to her another and bigger point that I was hung up on.

I can't fail her. And I almost had. If Tessa was making progress of adjusting to life after the trauma of being raped, I wasn't any better off. I constantly took hits of stress and guilt when I thought back to how I'd almost lost her. Seeing those two Giovanni men trying to break in and get to her arrested my heart, and I hated the mere thought of failing her. Of not looking out for her.

I'd failed my Mafia brothers, and I couldn't let it become a pattern and allow her to be wounded or killed as well.

Explaining any of that would be tricky, and until I knew how to approach the woman, I was determined to watch her from afar and let her come to me.

And finally, she did. When I walked past the hot tub later that night, grabbing my phone from where I'd left it at the rooftop terrace area where I'd sat and had a call with my father, she cleared her throat.

Seated—alone—in the swirling hot bubbles of the tub, she set her sights on me.

Fuck. Just the vision of her warm and wet... My self-imposed restraint would slip fast.

"Want to join me?"

Yes. Fuck yes. Yes a thousand times. "Should I?"

She nodded. "Please?"

I clenched my jaw, holding in a growl of desire. As I gazed into her dark-blue eyes and saw the longing in them, I lost control.

I'd been waiting for her to approach me, and with this invitation to soak with her, she had. I couldn't be choosy. I had to take the opportunities that arose, no matter how unlikely having a sincere conversation would be with us both lacking clothes and sharing the same space in water.

"Yeah. I'll join you." *Fuck me.* Just saying it felt like a risk. I only had sweats on over my swim trunks, having soaked earlier. I took them off and stepped in, feeling her gaze on me but refusing to make eye contact. If she was looking at me with smoldering desire that she didn't know how to act on, I'd be a goner. And I had to at least explain my hesitations before being stupid and giving in.

Sinking into the hot water felt good, but I was careful not to lower my arm all the way into the water. The bandages were minimal now, but I knew better than to expose the stitched area to the heated water.

"Romeo?"

Fuck, I love it when you say my name like that. Soft, slightly nervous, but braving it anyway.

"Yeah?" I opened my eyes and looked at her, noticing the signs of apprehension on her sweet face. Blonde strands stuck to her skin, and as she brushed them back, she licked her upper lip, teasing me without being aware.

"Are you…"

I tensed, waiting on the edge of my seat.

She inhaled deeply, making her breasts rise above the surface of the water. "Are you interested in me?"

20

TESSA

I didn't know how else to ask it. Coming right out with a direct question seemed both stupidly silly but also most appropriate. I felt juvenile, like I was back in junior high and asking if a cute boy in class *like* liked me. As adults, these sorts of things were simplified and implied.

Romeo seemed to want me. I caught him watching me when he must have thought I wasn't paying attention. I noticed how strained he was when I passed by too closely, daring to brush against him.

But everything was just so confusing. He made no moves. He didn't ask me anything intimate or personal.

We'd fallen into a strictly platonic roommate situation that felt so damn wrong. Like we were both dismissing this undeniable magnetism that kept us loosely together.

"Am I interested in you?" Romeo asked, returning my question to me over the steam rising from the tub. "How can you even ask that?" The hint of amusement in his tone almost made me smile. He wasn't mocking me but was incredulous that I posed that question to him.

I nodded, uncertain of speaking until I had his actual reply. All the pent-up tension and waiting had come—literally—to a boiling-over point as we sat in the hot tub together.

"I am. You've held my interest since the moment I saw you."

I furrowed my brow, thrown off by that comment. The first time he saw me was when I was helpless and raped. It didn't soothe me. If that first impression of my needing saving was the lasting one that he hinged his connection on, I had no hope.

"Oh."

"What's wrong, Tess?" he asked, quick to realize that I wasn't pleased with his response.

"Um." I cringed, hating that I'd said a single damn thing at all. I was an idiot to ever assume something more could happen between us. He was sweet and generous, but never intimate anymore.

Because I am *bad in bed?* I wasn't sure why that worry stuck at the front of my mind, like that had to be the reason he didn't want to sleep with me again. If it was good, or as pleasing as it had been for me, why wouldn't he want me again? I was here, always available. He never left my side, not since the shooting at the cabin.

If I had *any* experience before him, I bet I would at least have some confidence and knowledge to know how I measured. He'd gotten off. That had to count for something. But his lack of interest counted for a lot more, too.

"I..." I shook my head, intimidated to speak up now. I'd only stick myself further into a hold of regret.

"What?"

"Are you interested in keeping me here because I'm a responsibility?"

He stared at me, his hard face blank and shadowed under the night sky.

"That since I have no one else and nowhere else to go, you're obligated to take care of me and keep me here?" I licked my lips, finding more courage to get these thoughts off my chest. "That I'm a *thing* to take care of and make sure I stay unharmed?"

"No." He shook his head.

"You…" I sighed, pushed to reveal it all. "You had sex with me. But ever since, I've realized that you might not have wanted me at all. That you only went along with it because I was being needy and scared from my nightmares."

"No. I want you, Tess." He shifted in his seat in the hot tub. "I want you with every fucking breath I take."

"Because you have to?"

"Fuck. No, Tess. No one determines what I have to want or not want."

"But you've been so distant, and I don't know what to think."

"Think that I will be here to help you and take care of you."

Just not like that?

He didn't miss my instant wince. "I want you, Tessa, but I do *not* want to push you or pressure you."

Oh, my God. They were right. Nina and Eva said this might be the case, that Romeo didn't want to put pressure on me.

"You're still getting over the shock of what happened. Trauma isn't something that can just be swept away or dismissed. Yes, I want you, so fucking much it hurts, but I refuse to put you in a position that will make anything worse, in a position that will hinder how you can get through the trauma you suffered."

I nodded, both hating that he had to have that consideration and that I was ever raped, but also that he'd taken it to such an extreme of giving me *too* much space. Nothing about how we met was conventional, and

I was starting to realize that whatever—if anything—we built going forward wouldn't be conventional, either.

"Does that make sense?"

"It does. But I don't want you to hold me at arm's length." I stared at him through the haze of the rising steam and contemplated how to tell him that I wanted him to hold me close. "When I asked you to hold me, that... that helped a lot."

He sighed, dipping his chin to his chest for a moment. When he looked back up at me, I hated the guilt swarming in his eyes.

"That's my fault, Tess. I'm sorry that I've kept my distance, but it's something I am still trying to work on. This guilt."

"Guilt?" I shook my head, confused. "Guilt about what?"

"About many things. That I was the one who survived a fight when other Constella brothers died. That I failed to protect those men. It's fucking me up to realize how close I'd come to almost losing you and how I nearly failed at protecting *you* at that cabin."

This poor, tortured man. He was so serious, and like I'd suspected for a while now, he kept so much—too much—on his shoulders.

"But you didn't fail me. Not at all." I let loose an incredulous laugh. "I don't see how you ever can. You've been nothing but good and generous, so protective of me."

More than I probably deserve. In a fleeting moment of annoyance, I felt so greedy and self-centered. That every moment that I whined about him not wanting me, I was ungrateful for the security he so freely offered me without any expectations in return.

"If those men had come a moment sooner—"

"No." I shook my head. "We're not playing with *what-ifs*. Anything can happen, Romeo. Anywhere and anyhow. You can't predict the future.

You can't hold yourself accountable for everything that could go wrong."

Is that how he lives?

"Or is that part of the job description of being a Mafia prince? Expected to be in control, all the time?"

He looked at me so deeply, I wondered what was going through his mind. "I do like being in control."

"And when you're not, it's not easy to compromise?"

He shrugged his uninjured shoulder. "In psychobabble, that's probably a big part of it."

It seemed that he was summarizing a hell of a lot into one statement. *How long will you beat yourself up over this guilt for these things that you can't control?*

We both had issues. Him and his overprotectiveness and wanting to be in control. This guilt about failing. Then me with my tendency to shrink inside and manage the trauma of what those men did to me, rendering me a burden to be responsible for. I wanted him to see me as a desirable woman just for the sake of wanting *me*, who I was as a person, not a thing to handle or secure.

"Is there any chance you can set aside your guilt for me?"

My heart raced at the idea of showing him what I wanted. Excited and giddy, I debated acting on my desire, to show him who I was as a woman, not a responsibility to provide for, an aroused individual who refused to surrender to the fear of rejection.

He dragged his hot stare over me slowly, taking in the flesh that was bare above the water. His attention felt like a molten caress, and I needed to feel it everywhere.

"Any way you can focus on me and what we can have together?"

These words were foreign and risky on my tongue, but I didn't stop there. Standing in the middle of the hot tub, I rose out of the water. Rivulets of heated liquid streamed over me and left my skin chilled. When I untied my bikini top that I'd borrowed from Nina, my skin reacted with a spread of goosebumps.

"I can." His voice was husky and deep, full of need as he traced his gaze from my nipples pointing at him, up to my face. Holding his good arm out, he beckoned me to come closer. "Is that what you want?"

"I want you, Romeo. I've spent too many days and nights wondering why I was alone in this attraction—"

"You're not," he vowed as he tugged me the rest of the way until I fell in his lap. His erection thrust up at me, but I didn't have time to say anything. He slammed his lips to mine, kissing me hard and fast. "Not alone, Tessa. You never were."

He didn't make another move to kiss me, staring at me with such longing and impatience. But not budging.

"Then show me." I turned to straddle him, biting my lip at the pressure of his dick between my legs. "Show me that I'm not alone. That you want me too."

He opened his mouth to say something, but instead, he kissed me hard. For several long, torrid moments of his lips pressing against mine, I wondered if it was finally happening, that since I tried to speak with him directly, it opened the floodgates of truth. That he'd show me now how he desired me.

Or not.

His hands remained on the edge of the hot tub. His tongue dueled with mine, but only after I gestured that I wanted more. While he kissed me back and didn't stop me from grinding against his erection trapped in his shorts, he didn't seem like an eager or active participant.

"Romeo." I huffed, peeved and frustrated. "I don't understand. You say you want me, but you don't act like it."

He thrust his hips up. "I don't?"

I refused to be mocked. "You won't touch me. Or act… interested."

"I am, Tess. I am. But…" He looked away.

I framed his face until his eyes were locked on mine again. "But what? Tell me. You know I don't have experience. Explain to me why I should believe you when you say you're interested but act so… passive."

"I'm not a good man, Tess."

I rolled my eyes. "You are. To me. And that's all that matters." Yes, he killed people, but I was starting to understand that those murders were a matter of the ends justifying the means.

"I am a bad man."

I never hated my mother more. She called him that, and while I refused to think that was the first time he'd faced that criticism or judgment, it hit deep, somehow.

"And I am a hard man."

I furrowed my brow at him, trying to understand what that meant.

"I already explained that I prefer to have control. To be in control."

I dropped my arm. "Then take it."

"I don't do things like this. Light and soft and sweet."

I shivered under the intensity of his stare. "What do you mean?"

"I like it hard, Tess. Harder than what we did before."

Wicked fantasies filled my mind, but I couldn't lose the grip of confusion. Of feeling ignorant.

"Show me." I tipped my chin up, knowing I would meet him in the middle however he wanted me to. "Show me what *you* want, then."

21

ROMEO

"I want it all with you," I said honestly.

"Show me."

I'd never forget the sight of her so bold and determined, eyeing me like I was a challenge to take on.

"You're sure?" The thrill of exploring with her turned me on more. If she was serious, then I wouldn't waste a moment.

"Please, Romeo. Show me what you want."

I put my hands on her hips and loved the flinch of surprise she did at the contact. Like the sensation charged her.

"You want to be a good girl for me?" I teased, stroking my hands up and down her sides and reveling in the softness of her skin. "You want to be my good girl?"

She shook her head, looking at me from hooded eyes. "I want to be bad for you, Romeo. Make me bad."

Dirtying her up would be my fucking pleasure.

Bringing her closer, I welcomed the press of her hard nipples on my chest. "You're sure?"

She nodded, gazing at me intently as she came closer for a kiss. Her cheek brushed against mine as she curled against me. "I'm sure."

"Then stand up."

She did, bringing her black bikini bottoms to my eye level.

"Take them off."

Her fingers trembled as she untied to strings keeping the fabric up. My dick hardened, straining to be free, but I resisted the urge to react. I preferred the hard edge of this sort of push and pull, this thin line of trying to hold off from coming. It was almost a form of withholding orgasms for myself, but I'd only do it for her. To bring *her* the highest pleasure I could.

Yanking her down on me and fucking her fast would do the trick, but that was too easy.

"Hold it."

I stared at her pussy, bare and inches from my mouth as she stood there on the seat. Water lapped at her calves as she stood here, naked to the world. No one could see us this high up, but the air on her bare body had to be tormenting her and shredding her modesty.

Her fingers gripped the string as I reached for it. Kissing over her hips, I avoided bringing my lips to her pussy. No matter how much faster she breathed and regardless of how she tipped herself toward me, I refused to pleasure her there with my mouth.

Instead, kissing her lightly and revving up her anticipation for what could come, I tied her hands together behind her back. The bikini bottoms were no replacement for a binding, but the knots held. Her shoulders were pushed back and her hands rested at the small of her back. I cupped her hips, caressing over the globes of her ass until I had my hands on the backs of her thighs.

I gazed up at her, taking in every sexy inch of her, from her flat stomach to her heavy breasts, and the slenderness of her neck. Keeping a steady eye contact, I shifted to remove my shorts. She licked her lips, silent and tense, but so aroused, judging by the points of her nipples and her quick breaths.

"Come here." I guided her to kneel again, but I didn't bring her all the way down until she nudged my cock. I kept her up high on the seat that angled at a slope. Once her breasts were within reach, I leaned forward to sample her tits. Kissing, licking, and biting, I explored her sweet flesh, testing out how much pain and pressure she could take.

I didn't want anyone to ever mark her skin—except me. And I did. With my lips, teeth, and tongue, I tortured her flesh and gauged her reactions. She moaned and waved on her knees when I licked around her nipple, but she tensed and sucked in a sharp breath when I sucked hard on her and pulled her areola into my mouth.

She didn't resist the pain, and when I soothed the harder bites and sucks with my tongue, she groaned such a sexy sound that I growled in response.

"Do you still want me to show you?" I asked, staring at her lust-filled eyes as I lowered my hand over her stomach.

She nodded. "Please. Please, Romeo."

Surrendering was a complex process, but she was already doing so well in not moving her hands. It was a minimal form of bondage, but it was a decent start out here without any other resources or supplies.

"You want to be bad for me?"

"I want to be everything for you," she said huskily as I slipped two fingers into her pussy. I didn't trespass slowly or gently. Her arousal slickened her. She was already so wet, so warm but tight, and I hurried to scissor my fingers and take advantage of the speed of pushing into her. Last time, it was so slow and tender. Now, I demonstrated my hunger.

She cried out, arching into my hand. While I pistoned my fingers into her cunt, I doubled down in sucking at her tits, using my teeth to tug at her nipples too. Buoyed in the water and on the fine thread between pleasure and pain, she took it all.

"Get up," I ordered once she neared an orgasm. I felt the rising tension in her. I tracked her quick breaths that heralded her coming apart. It was too damn soon, and I kept her from coming.

"Romeo. Please!"

I smacked her ass and prompted her to stand.

It was a clumsy effort with her hands bound behind her, but I assisted her in getting up by keeping my hands on her hips. As soon as she was on her feet, I turned her and pulled her down. Holding my dick, I lined up to her pussy.

She cried out, arching her back as she remained over the water on my lap. With her hands bound behind her back, she had nothing to hold on to. Keeping her off balance was part of the thrill, and as I slanted deeper into the water, I drove up into her tight pussy with one long, hard thrust.

"Oh!" She gasped and moaned at being so full of me, and I didn't wait to instruct her.

"Ride me. Slide back on me and glove me with that fucking cunt. Right now."

She groaned, trying to ride me the best she could with her hands bound. Back and forth, she rocked through the water and squeezed me with her tightness.

Even though she was working at it, doing her best not to fall forward into the water like this, it wasn't enough friction. I was working with an amateur, but I didn't expect her to figure it out on her first try.

I held on to her as I lifted us out of the water. Seated on the edge of the hot tub, I waited for her to anchor her knees on the wooden platform. "I said ride me," I demanded as I began to untie the string from her wrists. The bikini bottoms stayed on one hand, but as soon as she could part her arms, she placed her hands on my knees and ground against me.

"Harder, Tess. Fuck me harder. Like you mean it."

She growled, curving her back and slamming down on me. Up and down, she bobbed on me, and I stared at her sweet ass, watching my glistening shaft disappear into her.

Pushing my hips up, I gave her a different angle. But when she faltered, so close to coming again, I slowed down my pushes to hold her off.

Too soon. It was way too fucking soon. For all that time we'd been denied each other, I refused to let this go too quickly.

Instead, I grabbed her hips and slid my hands over her ass. Once I squeezed her, gripping her hard, I brought my fingers along her crack.

She tensed, almost jerking off me completely, but I caught her in my arms before she slipped back into the water.

"No. No!" She shook her head, frantic. Her voice wasn't only a sound of protest, but fear. "Not—No!"

I gritted my teeth, hating that I'd caused her to panic. I should've known better, though, and I fought through the disappointment in myself that I hadn't made this all about pleasure for her. Going near her other hole likely triggered an unconscious fear. Something from when the men raped her.

And that wouldn't do. I hugged her to me, kissing her neck and easing her out of the panic. Keeping her focused on me, I reached up to bring her arms forward.

"I said ride me," I repeated, not letting her fall into her fears or memories.

"I—"

"Ride me," I ordered, glad that she'd never stopped all the way, still rocking her hips over me.

I wouldn't go near her ass again. And I didn't. As she rode me, I lowered one hand to rub her between her legs. I found her clit, and stimulating that had her nearing an orgasm again.

I succeeded in deterring her from freaking out about anything anal, but I wasn't ready to finish this. She gave me a good measure of what she could handle, and I was pleased that she was flexible to pain and impatience. It gave me hope that we could figure out a compromise.

"Turn around," I instructed.

"No. Please. I—"

"Turn. The. Fuck. Around."

She did, shakily and so clumsily that she almost fell.

As I leaned back further on the damp wood, I rested on my hands. The position didn't feel great with my gunshot wounds still healing, but once she straddled me again, sinking onto my dick, I groaned at the perfection of our bodies coming together like this. Like one.

"Pinch your nipples."

She lowered her gaze, watching my dick as she cupped her breasts, then did as I told her.

Last time was too tame. Under the covers, in the dark, and missionary. Like this, she proved that she could handle a lot more and enjoy it.

"Can I... Can I come now?" she whined, so sexy and needy.

"Now, Tessa. Now." I wouldn't last longer. Leaning forward, I held her back as I angled her to dip away from me. She didn't stop bouncing on my dick. And she didn't hold back on pinching and twisting her nipples. Once I lowered my fingers to her clit and rubbed there, she burst apart and clenched on my dick.

"Fuck. Oh, Romeo. *Fuck.*" She panted and wheezed, breathing so hard as her orgasm hit her. Under the tighter cinch of her pussy on my dick, I lost the willpower to deny myself any longer. With a sweeping rush of pleasure, I came. My cock jerked within her warm pussy, and I groaned as I flooded her with all my cum.

As she shivered and trembled from the overwhelming sensations, I gathered her close in my arms and carried her back into the hot tub. The hot water stung, but it also soothed. Together, hugging and so sated and spent, I rubbed her back and marveled at the gift of surrender she'd given me.

Then I wondered what else she'd want to offer next time. Because it would only get better and better if the deep, contented sigh she exhaled was anything to go by.

I kissed the top of her head, holding her close and knowing I was the luckiest man alive to be able to share such deep intimacy with her.

"Thank you," she mumbled, sleepily but conscious.

"For what?" I asked, still rubbing her back. If anyone should express thanks, it should've been me.

"Showing me how much… better it can be."

I chuckled and hugged her closer. "Are you saying it was bad the first time?"

Her cheek lifted in a smile against my chest. "No. Never. I enjoyed it then. But this was… more intense."

I kissed her temple. "What if I promised you that it could be even better?"

She shivered slightly and exhaled a long breath. "Then I would hold you to that promise. And look forward to when it could happen."

Fuck. You're perfect.

I tipped her face up and kissed her, sealing this moment with all the love I could ever have held in my cold, dark heart.

22

TESSA

A few days after I dared to tell Romeo to show me what he wanted, I headed over to the mansion where Dante and Nina lived. I was glad to be able to go somewhere, because after the nonstop days of having sex with Romeo and sleeping in his bed, I felt like I needed a reality check.

He showed me how hard he liked it. I let him test how much I could take with bondage. While it was likely a tame introduction to the kinky things he preferred, I was loving every second. He was patient but firm—always in control—and I was convinced that I had to pinch myself and know that it was real. That this was actually my life.

Seeing Nina was a treat, and when I saw that Eva was available as well, I looked forward to some honest-to-God girl talk while the men had their meeting.

"What do they need to talk about?" Eva asked as we watched them head to the patio. It seemed they preferred the table to the right. While it was a bit cooler, it wasn't too chilly to lounge out there.

We three set up in the great room, lying back on chairs and the couch.

"I think more about the bikers and Giovannis," Nina said with a shrug. "Always so much going on."

"Do you feel guilty?" I asked her. Since she was the catalyst to the bikers targeting the Constella Family, I had to wonder. When Dante pretended to be her boyfriend and thwarted Nina from going to Reaper, he started a hell of a fight.

"No. I did, but Dante likes to remind me that it wasn't my fault in the first place. It was Ricky's."

Eva waved at Nina. "And it's not like Stefan wasn't already causing trouble with my uncle." She rolled her eyes. "He's never really been that trustworthy. Not since he stood with the Domino Family before the MC tore them down."

I shook my head, wondering how Stefan Giovanni lived with himself. Befriending and allying one group, then after they were killed and ruined, teaming up with the enemy they fought? It sounded like an epic case of two-timing, and I didn't blame Dante and Romeo for not wanting to deal with the Giovannis.

"Enough about that." Eva set her wineglass down. "What's going on with you and my cousin?"

I blinked at her blunt question.

"Yeah." Nina grinned. "I've never seen him so…"

"Loose?" Eva guessed.

"Yeah." Nina looked pensive as she nodded. "More at peace, I guess."

"Because he's getting laid?" Eva guessed, glancing at me suggestively.

"Well…" My cheeks heated up, and I smiled as I looked at my water glass. "Yeah. He *is* getting laid."

"See!" Nina laughed. "I told you. Did you fess up and tell him what you wanted?"

"It was more like both of us talking and explaining a few things." I shrugged, shy yet not. This was the first time I'd ever contributed to a conversation like this. It was new. Fun. And freeing. I never could've done something like this in my former life, the nonstop working existence I suffered through before I met Romeo.

"Wow. I can totally see the difference in him," Eva said. "He's always been so serious, but just watching him here tonight, he's more relaxed somehow."

I rubbed my neck, wondering if I could really have that much impact on him. "I wonder how long it will last."

"What? Like how long the newness of it will last?" Nina asked.

"That too. But I mean how long he'll want me like this." Now my nerves crept in.

"What is *this*, though?" Eva asked. "Did he say? Or did you?"

I shook my head. "We haven't labeled it." *I wouldn't know how.* "We're basically living together and sleeping together. But…" I shrugged.

"That's a good start." Nina was still all smiles.

"But I don't know if I'm good enough to last."

Eva rolled her eyes.

"Hey, of course you are," Nina said, laughing me off.

"From the little I saw when you two arrived, he worships the ground you walk on, Tessa." Eva sounded so sure. I envied her confidence.

"A man doesn't look at a woman like that unless he's in deep," Nina said. "No pun intended."

We all giggled, smiling and having fun with the bawdy talk.

"It's just so new. And he's my first anything. First time having sex—when I wanted it." I grimaced at the reminder that I'd lost my virginity when I was raped. "If Romeo is my boyfriend, if that's the right label for him, he's my first."

"How naïve," Eva deadpanned.

Nina threw a decorative pillow at her. "Be nice."

"I'm honest," Eva argued.

"I am, though. Naïve. I can tell my inexperience is so not what he's used to." And I hated that feeling. I knew he'd had sex before. He was almost ten years older than me. Of course, he'd been around the block. "I don't mean the sheer amount of experience, comparing my history to his. It's more the…" I rolled my hand.

"What?" Nina asked, eager and on the edge of her seat.

"The *kind* of experience," I said, wincing and feeling less-than somehow. I wanted to please Romeo however I could, but I wasn't sure how to educate myself and be more prepared to impress him other than what he told me. I doubted a man wanted to coach their partner through *every*thing.

Other than that terrifying moment when his fingers near my ass made me tense up and struggle with triggered memories of being raped, I enjoyed all that he pushed me to feel. Surrendering to him was liberating somehow, but I got the sense that he wanted more.

"Oh." Nina furrowed her brow. "I think I know what you mean. Romeo's so… intense and serious." She nodded and glanced at Eva, as though seeking confirmation from someone who'd known him longer. "He'd be a hard lover, I'm guessing. More serious than playful."

Eva hummed in agreement. "I know exactly what you mean," she confided in me, again with that firm confidence that she had no matter what she talked about. She wasn't light and fluffy. The stunning brunette was almost as serious as Romeo seemed to be.

"He's a *dark* kind of lover," she summarized. "He used to go to clubs with Franco."

I winced. "Sex clubs?" I'd never measure up to the kinks there.

"Yeah. BDSM, too, but he wasn't that hardcore, I don't think." She held up her hands in surrender and tilted her head to the side. "My cousin's—and uncle's—sexual appetite is none of my business. Please, never mistake my willingness to chat about this in a general sense for an invite to unload details."

Nina smiled, fighting back laughter.

"But I understand what you mean," Eva commiserated. "I imagine that Romeo would just show you what he wanted and all."

"Oh, he does. And he is. But I feel like needing the instruction makes me less-than."

Nina blew a raspberry. "Nah. If he's a control freak like I think he is, he'd take pleasure from 'teaching' you."

"He does."

"You've read books," Nina said with a wink. "Including one-hand romances."

"There you go." Eva nodded and finished her wine. "Watch some porn and learn a little more."

I leaned over in my seat, resting my elbows on my knees. I was intrigued and excited. The thrill of doing something so naughty like watching porn... I grinned. "Like what, though?"

"Hmm. Anal?" Eva guessed. "That's pretty basic and a common kink."

I refrained from wincing. I wasn't sure I could adjust to that.

"Bondage. Maybe some flogging and stuff. Romeo's never gotten *that* involved with the club scene, but I wouldn't be surprised if his tastes still veered toward the dark side."

"Thanks, Eva." I smiled at Nina, too. "This helps. I was trying not to feel insecure, being so new to this and so soon after being..." I exhaled a long, hard breath. Voicing it out loud was simply something that would take more time.

"Glad to help," Eva said. "However, no more details are necessary. Got it?"

"Got it." I smiled, shifting into more general talk about how Nina's pregnancy was going and how Eva was sick of some of the Mafia men who "wasted her time". As intelligent and wise as she was, she sure seemed impervious to considering a love life of her own.

It wasn't my place to ask her about why she wasn't seeing anyone. I was hardly an expert myself, only a couple of weeks in with the man I assumed it was safe to call my first boyfriend.

I couldn't help but feel like I was sheltered. My parents had never encouraged me to be a feminist or to date boys. They'd had it in their heads from so early on that I should be with Elliot.

Now, though, as I embraced being Romeo's woman, I fell deeper under the spell of curiosity, wondering what it would be like to look into the kinkier stuff that would please Romeo.

Because already, this soon, I knew that when I gave my submission to him and he led me with control, he made me soar so high with bliss that I doubted I'd ever want it to stop.

I wasn't sure what I ever did in my life to deserve him or how he treated me, but I didn't want to consider it ever ending.

No more stress about having to work nonstop, only to give my money to my parents. No more wondering how I could have a semblance of independence. No more dreading a call or text from Elliot that I'd need to reply to while not giving him any encouragement or hope.

All I had to do was enjoy Romeo treating me like a queen.

And pray that he got the same soul-deep satisfaction being with me that I did with him.

23

ROMEO

The more that I healed from being shot, the busier I became. Not only with Tessa and her eagerness to have sex with me on my terms, but also with the family.

It was too easy to assume it was just me and her, the two of us, and that nothing else mattered. In the penthouse so high in the sky, it sometimes felt like it was just us alone, on top of the world and untouched by any outside influences.

Meeting with my father and Franco proved otherwise.

"That motherfucker is going to regret the day he ever dared to set foot on our turf," my father growled, pacing near the table out near the pool that was already being serviced for the fall closing procedure.

Stefan Giovanni was ramping up his attacks. Just this morning, he had his goons set fire to one of our businesses. It was "just" a bakery and deli. That was what it would look like in the news. To all who knew what was what, Stefan had tried to take out one of our well-operated drug packaging sites. The entire basement level of that building was where we had drugs packaged for dealers.

Fortunately, no one was in there when the fire was lit. No deaths. And with a transitional step between deliveries, not much product was lost in the fire, either. Still, it was a pain in the ass to deal with. Paying off the fire marshal to look the other way about evidence. Reducing the rumors spread about what happened. All of it.

Franco groaned and rubbed his face. "But we still won't handle it if they attack from two sides. Stefan's well versed on how to cause trouble for us, but those goddamn bikers are a whole other issue. They won't play by the same rules, and we risk being outnumbered."

My father paced again, shaking his head. "I know. But it's fucking bullshit."

We weren't being cowardly about retaliating, but wise about it. Rushing into anything with guns blazing wouldn't equal glory.

"He'll feel the heat when we foil his plans with the MC, then," I said, already laying out the ways we could fuck with them. Andy continued to give me intel, and I put it to good use now. All that spying would benefit us.

After that meeting, my work time took over my opportunities to fuck Tessa and simply enjoy having her close. I was glad that she never lacked for anything to preoccupy herself. If she wasn't reading or texting with Nina, she was cleaning. The penthouse didn't get that dirty with just the two of us, but I noticed that she liked things tidy. Perhaps it was a residual effect of her always having jobs, a built-in or trained neat-freak tendency. She might have come across like a clingy woman to others, but she wasn't lazy or spoiled. Her baking attempts were precious disasters, but I appreciated that she had her own interests.

Having to go into the city and meet with the men more often wasn't a hardship, but now that I had Tessa in my life, I wanted the ability to make her my whole life. She might still be falling for me, but I'd fallen first. And hard. It was only her inexperience and recent rape trauma that kept me at a more mild-mannered pace with her.

A week after the fire, I came home later than I wanted. Every time I arrived at the penthouse, I looked forward to seeing her and letting her welcome me home.

"Any issues?" I asked the two men who stood stationed at the door.

"Nope." Both nodded at me as I entered.

Once I closed and locked the door, though, I suspected that wasn't the case. I had a very big issue on my hands.

I froze, narrowing my eyes at the sounds I heard coming from the bedroom. Groans and moans. The sounds of pleasure.

"Take it, slut. You take it hard for me," a man ordered.

What the fuck? Anger filled me that I could've been so mistaken about Tessa.

And the issue of those useless guards at the door, letting another asshole in here to be with her?

I ran, pulling my gun from my holster.

As soon as I skidded to a stop in the bedroom we shared, I caught my breath. Then I blinked my eyes and took in what was happening.

Tessa wasn't cheating.

No man told her to take it hard in here.

She was watching porn. A woman and a man. He fucked her mouth while she rode a dildo.

A smile tugged at my lips. I was amused that she hadn't registered that I'd come in the room. But I quickly became intrigued, so curious that she'd choose something like this for her viewing pleasure. It wasn't like I didn't give it to her regularly. "Lonely?"

She squeaked, startled and scrambling onto her knees from lying on her stomach on the bed. The laptop slid off the edge of the bed with her jostling around, and I had to bite the inside of my cheek to hold in a laugh at her dismay and embarrassment.

Her cheeks were red, and she fumbled not to fall off the bed as she dove for the laptop. Facing me sheepishly, she pulled her lips in and exhaled hard through her nose.

"No," she admitted dryly. "I'm not lonely."

"Really?" I put my hands in my pockets to hold back from lunging at her and fucking her wildly.

"How could I be lonely when I have you in my life?"

"Hmm." I stepped closer.

"But I realize now that you've been holding out on *me*."

I raised my brows. "Is that so?"

She nodded as she dropped to her butt and sat on the mattress. "I know I'm… new to all this. The things you might like."

I leaned forward and set my hands on the bed, stalking toward her. "Things I might like?" I kissed her softly. "I like *you*, Tessa." *I fucking love you.* But I doubted she was ready to hear that.

"The dark stuff. Kinky stuff."

"What gave you the idea that I want things like that?"

She looked me up and down, interest clear in her eyes. "Well… You said you didn't do things light and soft."

"I think I've proven that I can, but I prefer not to. My life isn't light and soft."

She nodded, lowering her legs as I hovered over her. It was intoxicating, feeling like I was trapping her right in place where I wanted her to be. Under me. Submissive to me. Craving me.

"Eva mentioned that you used to go to clubs."

That snitch. I nodded. I wasn't ashamed of my past. It was what it was. I doubted I'd ever bring Tessa to one for the simple matter of not wanting anyone else to see her. She was *mine*.

"And I thought maybe I could educate myself more and watch some…"

"Educational material?" I teased.

She pursed her lips, pouting. "Don't make fun."

"If I want you to learn something more advanced than vanilla sex," I said as I gave her a slow once-over, "I'll show you myself."

She sighed, and just that breathy sound made my dick harder. Like she was struggling with her desire for me. Like she was battling intense feelings and unsure how to express it.

"I only wanted to impress you."

I reached for her neck and gripped the back of it to haul her closer. After I kissed her quiet, getting the reward of her pliant and lax under my fingers, I gazed at her dark-blue gaze that never failed to captivate me.

"I am very impressed," I promised. "But let me have a look at you again."

She grinned, catching on quickly that I was in the mood to play. Leaning back on her hands, she shifted her stance on the bed until she tugged off the low-cut tank top. Then came her shorts. And that was it. She lay before me completely naked. No panties or bra, almost as though she was eagerly waiting for my arrival and not wanting too many layers preventing us from being naked together the moment I got home.

"Extremely impressive," I commented as I lowered toward her. She fell back in sync with my dip down. Once she lay flat on the bed, I closed my mouth around her tit and sucked hard. Hard enough to turn her flesh red and her nipple pointed like a bead. "Absolutely gorgeous when I see my marks on you."

She sighed, another one of those long, sexy-as-fuck, drawn-out moans of pleasure. This woman would be the death of me, and it bothered me that she thought she was lacking. That she wasn't impressing me and wowing me already. No flaw could turn me off. I, however, had numerous red flags that should've sent her running. The fact that she hadn't yet, and didn't seem inspired to, made my heart sing.

Wait. What did she say? She hadn't complained, but she'd worded it in such a way that gave me pause.

"What do you mean that I'm holding back on you?"

"Well, seeing some of the things in those videos…" She reached up to frame my face. Loving the feel of her soft hands on me—anywhere—I turned to kiss her palm, then her wrist. As I pushed her arm up, she followed suit with the other. She was a quick learner, already knowing that when I indicated for her to lift her arms, it meant she was supposed to keep her hands up and out of the way so I could dictate what would happen.

"What about them?"

"I, um…" She lost track of her words as I alternated between her breasts, kissing and sucking hard.

"What about them?" I prompted again after a more forceful tug on her wet nipple.

She hissed. "I… I wouldn't mind trying some of those things."

She needed to clarify. We'd experienced oral, both of us giving and receiving. She was open to bondage, but I had yet to scale up any harder with her.

"Which things?" All I knew for a fact was that she didn't want anything anal, which was a shame, but we'd work on it eventually. "I hope you understand that I have been trying not to overwhelm you."

She nodded as I stepped back and started to remove my shirt. Her gaze was locked on me, tracking the movement of my fingers as I undid the buttons one by one. "You were a virgin until recently," I reminded her unnecessarily. Of course, she fucking knew that. But sometimes, I worried she was overzealous in wanting to shed that former identity and force herself to be this born-again sex goddess.

"I know. And I appreciate your trying to ease me into all this."

I discarded my shirt. "And with what you had to endure just before we met, I've been trying my best not to push you too far."

She smiled, soft and sweet as I started to remove my pants and boxers.

"The last thing I want to do is lose control in going for what I'm used to and overstimulate you. I want to go gradually and let you set the pace of what you want with me, of what you're willing to try." *Or interested in.*

"But I am willing. To try." Her throat flexed with a difficult swallow, belying her nerves. Yet, I knew she was telling the truth. "To please you. I want to be the woman you want and deserve, Romeo."

"You *are* the woman I want," I told her earnestly as I set my knee on the bed, wedging it between her legs. I ran my fingertips up along her inner thigh toward her pussy, and I was rewarded with a faint tremor and spread of goosebumps. She was always so responsive to my touch, and I prayed she always would be.

"And while a lot of this is new," she continued bravely, looking me in the eye, "I *am* curious. I wish you could try to show me more."

I would never hear sweeter words. "Like what?" I didn't miss how she was asking me to show her, respecting that I would still be in control. Tess was magnificent when she trusted me enough to let go and submit to me, and as long as she learned that dynamic, she could be confident that I would always adhere to seeing to her pleasure above all else, no matter what it took to get her there.

"Specifically?" Her cheeks turned pink, and I was both humored and amazed that she could still blush after all we'd done.

I thought back to what the video was playing when I walked in. A woman blowing a man while he had a toy in her cunt. "Toys?"

She pulled her lips in and nodded slightly. "I mean, I watched a lot of videos before that one, but yeah. I would like to try more, um, accessories."

"You want to be my bad girl and play with some toys, huh?" I taunted her, loving how she reacted to filthy talk and slight degradation. It never failed to make her slick and needy. I didn't pause to feel her and test how wet she was. Instead, I stood up and rounded the bed.

She kept her hands above her head, clasps together and so obedient not to move them away until I might tell her to. But she tracked me, staring at my dick as it jutted out. I walked around the bed until I was on the other side. Once there, I dragged her by her arms to position her at the edge.

"I'm going to fuck that sexy mouth," I told her.

As I raised my dick to her parted lips, I teased her according to the video that I'd interrupted her watching. "And you're going to take it."

She moaned as I pushed my hips forward and fed my cock into her mouth. Wet, warm, and tight, she sucked her cheeks and quickly slid over me.

I watched, mesmerized just like every time she sucked me off. Back and forth, I humped her face. And deeper and deeper, she swallowed me in.

As I fucked her face, loving how she stretched to accommodate me and breathed hastily through her nose to keep up with the motion, I leaned to the side to open the middle drawer of my bed. I ordered these the first day we came here, just hoping that they'd be used. I liked to be prepared, and I was fucking glad I'd hoped and planned accordingly. The night had come to introduce Tessa to the world of vibes, dildos, and other "accessories", as she'd called them.

I grabbed the first vibe I could find and stepped closer to the bed. With her diagonal on the mattress, it wasn't too hard to change my position and slide her to where I wanted her.

After a few drags of the vibe over her creamy pussy, I nudged the tip against her hole. She moaned, and the vibration traveled up my dick as I sank in deeper yet, nearly gagging her.

I stared at her cunt, her folds opening to accommodate the vibe that I had yet to turn on. I'd only set it to her entrance, and already, I knew that *I* would be the one struggling to handle it.

"Are you going to take this, too?" I teased as I prepared to mimic the porn she was watching.

A longer, affirmative moan came from her mouth stuffed with my dick. Choking on me like this, she couldn't say anything else.

"Oh, you are bad." She wasn't. She was simply perfect, an eager lover ready to explore with me.

I smiled in anticipation for all I'd be able to teach her tonight.

24

TESSA

It was embarrassing for Romeo to come home and catch me red-handed, watching a porn. That humiliation hadn't lasted long, though. And now that it seemed like he wanted to re-enact what I was viewing, I was so damn glad that I'd taken Eva's advice to "research" with porn.

He hovered over me, but with the slight side angle that I lay in, he wasn't suffocating me. His dick prevented me from breathing better, but I loved the thrill of having my mouth stuffed with his hard yet smoothly soft penis. So salty. So thick. I reveled in contours and the ridges of his veins, and every time that tight flesh slipped over my lips, the friction of the contact made me more aroused. Getting turned on from pleasing him was such an extra reward, and I would never stop trying to impress him, to excite him and deliver him immense pleasure.

The sensation of the long, hard object at my pussy was different. Instead of his shaft or his fingers easing into my wet entrance, it was something hard and foreign. But not bad. Having him watch something get sucked into me there was a filthy idea. Sloppy, sluicing noises came with his pushes into my pussy, and the naughty sounds of how damn wet I was made me drip even more.

The things this man did to me. It blew my mind and rocked my body. My heart wasn't much safer. Romeo completed me like the other half I hadn't known I was searching for. And his dominance was the guidance I hadn't realized I needed to properly let go and just *be*. To feel.

In and out, he slid the thick dildo. Slower but steadier with his thrusts into my mouth, he replayed the actions that I had been watching on the screen. A cock ramming into my mouth until my eyes watered. A dildo slipping into my pussy to make me wriggle and arch up into his hand and the toy.

"You take it, Tess," he demanded as he activated the toy. It buzzed, stimulating my sensitive flesh all that much more, and I lost my rhythm of sucking him into my mouth. Almost gagging, I blinked through the tears and moaned my ultimate pleasure and surprise.

He stopped thrusting into me so hard as he leaned lower. Still not crushing me with his weight since I was slightly on my side, he switched things up from what I watched in the porn. With his dick seated in my mouth, the vibe deep in my pussy, he arched over to suck on my clit.

I moaned, muffled with his dick in my mouth, but he remained deep in me as he leaned his thighs against the edge of the bed.

"Hold on to me and fuck me," he ordered when he paused to lift his mouth from my clit.

I didn't wait. Holding on to his thighs, I gave leverage to bob my head on him, craning my neck to make the fit work. Once I got going, he put his mouth back on me. His tongue didn't stop once, circling my clit. He resumed working the vibe into my pussy, faster and harder. But it was his kisses to my bundle of nerves, suctioning to the point of pleasure and pain mixed into one.

I came quickly, splintering apart as the bliss shot through my veins. From my toes to the top of my head, I felt frazzled and jolted, as though this orgasm had the potential to carry an electrical charge.

With his dick crammed into my mouth, I couldn't do much more than moan longer and louder. I didn't know if he thought I was voicing anything negative, but the need to catch my breath stopped me from speaking up when he pulled his hips back and deprived me of making him spurt his cum down my throat.

"Don't move." He walked around the bed, leaving the vibe between my legs. It wasn't on, but just the presence of it in my pussy had my orgasm continuing in smaller waves of pleasure.

After he lay on his side, facing me and tucking me almost flush against him, he lifted my leg and draped it over his. He kissed me so hard and long that I swore I'd pass out. But if I did, it'd be one hell of a blissful way to go. At the same time he made out with me, letting me taste myself on his tongue while he sampled his muskiness on mine, he lowered my hand between us.

Once my fingers bumped into the vibe, I jolted at the deeper push. Then with his fingers curling mine around it, I caught on to what he wanted. I held the handle and followed his lead to thrust it in and out.

"Oh, fuck, Romeo." I groaned, resting my head back on the pillows. Overwhelmed with such an addicting friction, I felt the sensitive drag of the toy on my inner walls.

"Nice and slow, Tess." He rubbed his hand over my ass, and after he dipped his finger in my hole *with* the vibe inside, he moved his digit back to my ass.

I tensed, but when I opened my eyes and saw him watching me with patience and concern, I knew he had been waiting for it.

"I—"

He kissed me softly. "Trust me."

I winced as he probed around my back entrance. "I do, but I don't know…"

"Keep your hand moving," he said when I faltered.

Steady and with gentle force, he smeared my cream around my rear hole. While the memories of what those men did taunted me, I did my best to fight through it all.

"Look at me," he urged with another kiss. "Focus on what *you* are doing."

I moaned as the vibe stretched me.

"This is just you and me. No one else. Focus on me. On you. On *us*."

I closed my eyes and leaned in to kiss him, needing that simple but powerful contact. These kisses with him were the sharpest contrast, the grounding touch that always pulled me out of the past and stayed in the present. My rapists hadn't attempted intimacy. They'd only violated. Romeo, though, was my lover, giving me such tender affection and pushing me to broaden my horizons with him.

Over and over, I worked the dildo into my overstimulated pussy. And around and around, he massaged at my hole.

When he probed his finger, pressing into me, I stiffened again, but with another hasty kiss on his lips, I fell back into the moment. The hot, taboo, but surprisingly thrilling moment with him.

"You can take it, huh?" he asked, not goading me but checking.

I replied by lifting my leg higher over his.

Pleasure, so hot and new, filled me with his touches where I was taught no one should ever go. No normal lover would want to be in my ass at all. That was what the rigid sex education I'd received told me.

With his finger pumping into my ass while I pistoned the dildo in and out of myself, I was so close to a brutal orgasm that I feared I wouldn't be put back together again. The bliss would be too strong. The sensation of flying and floating and sinking and drowning—all at once—would short circuit me.

"You're going to take it and come, Tess." He kissed me harder as he pulled his finger out of my ass. On a pull out of the dildo, he collected more of my juices and slid two fingers in my ass.

"Oh…" While the toy was almost out, his dick came closer.

"Put my dick in your pussy," he ordered as he kissed and sucked on my neck. His fingers didn't stop in my ass, and without the dildo in there and tightening the pressure, I was impatient to be stuffed full again.

I lined him up and braced myself for his thick cock to fit in me. With an instant slam in, he was seated. Between his dick and his fingers, both my holes stuffed, I cried out at the nearness of the orgasm that I was sure would break me.

"Watch me," he ordered.

I opened my eyes and stared into his. The light blue was so bold and vibrant, flashing so hot and fierce.

"Watch me as I make love to you."

I nodded, kissing him quickly because I needed his lips on me.

"Watch me as I fuck your tight cunt." He pounded into me harder.

"As I keep my fingers in your sweet ass." He growled, so close to coming himself.

"Give it to me, Romeo," I begged as he worked in and out of me. My mouth hung open as I frantically pulled in air to breathe. "I want you. I want it all."

"Fuck!" He furrowed his brow, staring at me and straining to push me over the edge of tortuous buildup to relief.

A moment later, he did. Every nerve ending felt frayed, and with a pulsing rush of bliss so sweet and potent that I cried, I came. My pussy clenched his hardness that jerked and spilled his cum so deep inside me. The muscles in my ass tightened as he continued to stroke his fingers. Together, we came. His release seemed to be a hard and blindingly brutal one like mine. I didn't have much to compare to, but I had never, ever come so hard in my life.

After he pulled his fingers out of me and slid out, his dick smearing our cum on my thigh, we lay there panting and gasping for air.

For a long while, I came down from the high snuggled against him. Words weren't necessary. Speech was impossible. All we could do was lie there and recover our breath as our hearts slowed back down.

My entire body was numb with bliss. My arms and legs felt leaden with a heaviness that had me giving up the idea of anything but sleeping.

He didn't let me. Eventually, he urged me to slide over so he could stand. While I lay there and smiled, too whipped and satisfied to even think about moving, he went into the bathroom and cleaned up. He returned with a wet cloth and cleaned me up. Then he climbed right back into bed and hugged me close.

Stroking his hand over my back, he sighed deeply. Between the comfort of his hard, hot body, the security of his hug as tender aftercare, and the soothing sensations of his hand rubbing back and forth on me, I drifted closer and closer to sleep.

Before I gave in to the lure of a deep rest, I figured we would talk about these new steps we'd taken tomorrow. Any talking could wait. After that heated trial of sex, passing out was all we could handle.

But he had to have the last word.

"I love you, Tessa."

His voice was so low, so soft, that I couldn't tell whether I was dreaming or not. And with the next deep rise and fall of his chest beneath my cheek, suggesting that his even breath meant he was already checked out, I wondered if he'd said it consciously or not.

25

ROMEO

With the help of Nina and Eva, Tess easily adapted and fell into her role as my woman. They were critical in answering her many questions about who was who and what happened with the Domino Family, the Giovannis, and even the bikers.

The Constella organization had ample enemies. For many generations, we'd fought plenty of others who wanted the power we'd amassed and funneled into more wealth and dominance. They would never beat us, but I understood how Tessa might feel lost with all the names tossed around and the rumors that could be shared about what happened when and where, and how it could cause ripples of consequences. A crash course wouldn't be enough, but I was glad that Nina and Eva were available to help Tessa fit in.

One such night, when we came to the mansion so I could meet with my father and Franco, I caught snippets of what the women chattered about in the kitchen. Over coffee and cake, they gossiped and joked around to the point that I had to refrain from laughing.

"I'm just saying," Nina teased. "When Dante and I are married, I'll be Romeo's stepmom."

I rolled my eyes. Technically, I supposed she would be. But it wouldn't mean anything or change anything.

Eva laughed harder. "And then when you marry—"

"If," Tessa argued.

"If and when you marry Romeo," she went on, "you would become Nina's stepdaughter-in-law."

I smiled from my seat in the other room, where they must have assumed I couldn't hear them. The idea of marrying Tessa filled me with pride and joy. She already felt like my wife. We lived together. I provided for her. We slept together and shared as much intimacy as we could. I was damned proud of her for overcoming her fear of anything anal, and the fact that she could showed how much she trusted me.

Marrying Tessa would be in the plans. I wasn't sure when or how to make it happen, but I would. There was no doubt in my mind that we would be together forever, and looking forward to it gave me the ultimate sense of purpose.

"I'm not sure that'll ever happen," Tess said, slightly dejected.

I furrowed my brow. What the fuck?

"I have no clue what we're doing or who I am to him. A girlfriend? A kept woman?"

I sighed heavily, happy that she didn't say she was a goddamn burden. I'd fucked that idea out of her.

"The men in the family don't really bother with titles and labels," Eva said. "You're married or not, so you're a wife or a girlfriend. Even though one is a legal binding, they're basically the same and you'll be treated the same."

Nina made a noise of disagreement. "I'm not sure about that. Didn't you say that the Domino Family was notorious for swapping mistresses to spy on their own members?"

"Well, yes. There's the whole thing with mistresses, too, but no one really deals with that in the Constella Family," Eva replied.

"No," Tess said, "it's not the label. It's more like I don't know what he thinks. And I don't want to be petty and ask, but it doesn't matter. I don't have a job. I don't have my own place."

"And your parents took all your money," Nina added, annoyed and aggravated.

"That's bullshit," Eva said. "Dante or Romeo can fix that."

"What!" It sounded like Tess spat out her wine.

"They can get your money back. Romeo will do you right, regardless of not putting a label on you," Eva said. "Or putting a ring on it."

"Yet," Nina added, teasing.

I damn well would put a rock on her finger. While I was upset to hear Tessa still be so worried, assuming that I wouldn't take care of her, I understood it. She was independent, and if the roles were reversed and I was the one who'd suddenly gotten swooped up in all this, I would feel the same. Instead of being insulted and viewing this in the light of her not trusting me, I was glad that she was so practical and still had a self-sufficient mindset. She wasn't the typical Mafia wife, clingy and lazy, dependent on a man for everything.

"It's all tip money and such," Tess said. "For years. There is no way anyone could easily quantify it all and, what, sue them for it?" She huffed.

I smirked. You want to bet, my good girl? If she ever wanted me to recoup all the money that she gave her parents, I would make it happen. I'd demand that they pay her back—with interest—but I suspected she'd want as little contact with them as possible.

After the way that her mother yelled at her in the hospital, I doubted Tessa wanted to ever be in her presence again. I would always make that my mission, to protect her from them, from anyone.

I need to speak with them and tell them to fuck off for good. Tessa was my girlfriend. My lover. My future bride. Maybe one day, the mother of my children. She was my future, and I would never be so careless as to let her past interfere with her moving forward with me.

Killing them seemed extreme, but I would do her right. Justice was justice.

Nina switched the topic to her baby shower, and while Tessa was all about the conversation, Eva excused herself. Her heels clicked and clacked over the marble floor as she went from the large kitchen toward the great room I sat in.

I looked up from idly scrolling on my phone and caught her noticing me. True to her cool nature, she didn't jump or flinch. We both knew I was listening, and she wouldn't apologize or make excuses for it. Eva was consistent like that, unruffled, always "on" and maintaining the air of never letting anything bother her. Deep down, I knew she was more feeling and receptive. She had to be, but not much could penetrate the icy shell she hid behind.

"I'm grateful that you and Nina can help Tessa adjust to our lifestyle."

She sat, arching one brow. "Nina and me?" She twisted her lips in a wry smirk. "I wouldn't say Nina's an expert herself. She's still learning."

I chuckled. Fair enough. "You know what I mean. I'm glad that Tessa can ask you questions and count on you as resources."

She nodded. "I admit that she's surprised me. Coming from a shitty background, and then the incident of the night you found her… She's a tough one. You've done well to stick with her."

I raised my brows. "Implying that I don't have staying power otherwise?"

"Sort of. You've never had a relationship longer than a week, and here you are, looking like you're the most besotted man on earth." She huffed a light laugh. "Other than your dad, I suppose."

"It's not complicated."

She furrowed her brow. "Oh, sure."

"It's not. When you meet the other half of your soul, everything falls into place." I was generalizing a lot. Nothing had simply fallen into place for me and Tess. I had to work on getting over my guilt. She had to cope with the trauma of being raped. We both had to manage the pent-up tension and self-denial we'd suffered those weeks of not communicating clearly. It had taken effort on our part to come together, but now that we had, I knew nothing could stop us from sharing our love.

"Are you listening to yourself? Where'd my super-serious and gloomy cousin go?" She smiled as she teased, so I wasn't bothered. "You've saved your Cinderella girl and are over the moon to treat her so well. It's quite the one-eighty you've done there."

I shrugged, not in any mood to deny it. "Who knows, maybe you'll be next."

She deadpanned at me. "Yeah, right."

"Why not? Maybe love is just in the air."

"Love?" She smiled, a sweet and slow one. "You love her?"

I shot her a look that implied that she was being stupid. "Of course."

"But if she knew that, she wouldn't be in there"—she jerked her thumb toward the kitchen—"wondering how much she matters."

"We haven't shared those words yet, but yes, I love her." So fucking much I could burst. I pointed at her. "Nice try, changing the subject. You very well could be next to settle down."

She shook her head, letting her long, brown hair fall over her shoulder. "No man would ever want me."

It wasn't low self-confidence that she was arguing with, but realistic high confidence. "No man would ever want the challenge of putting up with me."

I sighed. My cousin knew her worth. She never flaunted it, but she was aware that she was gorgeous, a bombshell of a woman men lusted after. More than that, she was intelligent and sharp.

"I'm too rare, Romeo. A Mafia princess, remember?"

Her wording would make her seem full of herself, but I knew her better than that. She simply didn't suffer fools.

"For one thing, I'm not afraid to be assertive. And no man will enjoy that for long."

She always had to be assertive, and my father raised her the same as he had me—instilling a deep sense of confidence and will, making sure we were both smart and capable to survive in this world prone to danger and drama, full of lies and deceit.

Seeing my father finally enter the room, I stood to start this meeting. Franco would be around sooner or later, and then, I could spend the rest of the night showing my girl how I loved her. Tessa would hear the words from me soon, but I wanted it to be the perfect moment.

"Don't worry, Eva," I said as I stood.

"Does it look like I'm worried?"

She didn't look bothered at all, but beneath that cool mask, I bet she was feeling the effects of slight envy as my father and I settled with our women.

"Someone is bound to show up in your life and make you change your mind about being single."

I gave my father a chance to stop in the kitchen to kiss Nina before our meeting. As I headed to the patio, I ran into Franco as he arrived. We were always busy, going from one thing to another, but he slowed to walk with me to the table outside.

"I found some more info about your lawyer," he said after we greeted each other.

"My lawyer?" The family had an extensive web of legal support, but none of us had a specific representative.

"Hines. The slimy bastard who is supposed to marry your girl?" He looked at me, almost amused that I couldn't read his mind and immediately know what he was talking about.

"Good or bad info?"

He shrugged as we continued outside. "Just intel. He's got his hands in so many pies it's getting messy. Both Reaper and Stefan lean on him, and I think going after him would turn over a lot of stones we haven't considered."

"I don't want to prolong a crusade against him," I said. "But I do intend to meet with him. I don't want anything—anyone—to stand in my way with Tess."

"Don't blame you." He took a seat and frowned. "You're not thinking he's got some kind of signed document with her parents that she'd marry him, do you?"

I thought back to the whiny, judgmental woman in the hospital, the woman who called herself Tess's mother. "No. I doubt they've put anything formal into play. If they have, I'll eliminate it."

He nodded. "Just let me know how I can help."

"Thanks." He didn't have to offer, and I wouldn't have to ask. That was how we worked, together as a family, looking out for each other. I grew excited about Tessa learning that she had a family in us all, a support network unlike anything she'd ever dreamed of having before.

Franco huffed a single sarcastic laugh. "You're not going to ask her old man for permission to marry or anything like that, are you?"

I gave him a droll look.

He cracked up. "Yeah. I didn't think so."

I didn't intend to ask Mr. West for anything. Tess wasn't his to give away. She could make up her own mind and decide if she wanted to marry me. But Franco gave me the idea to at least reach out to Mr. and Mrs. West.

Not to announce my interest in marrying her.

But to tell them that she was mine.

They would never upset her or try to manipulate her again.

No one would. If anyone dared to harm a single hair on her head or incite the slightest worry in her mind, they would pay dearly. I would stop at nothing to prevent her from suffering, and I refused to let any obstacle get in the way of what would be our bright future.

26

TESSA

The next time I went to the shooting range to practice with the gun Romeo had given me, I met with Max, an older soldier who was missing three of his fingers on his non-dominant hand. He was tortured by enemies and barely made it out alive, but he had. And he was, according to Romeo, the Constellas' expert marksman.

Romeo was too busy to practice with me today, the same as every day this week, but he told me that I was in good hands with Max.

I was. Not only was he informative, but he was also personable and chatty in a non-obtrusive way. I realized my concentration was much improved, too, because every time I came here with Romeo, he'd sneak up close to me to demonstrate how to hold or fire my gun, which would tempt me with his proximity. Having my man's arms around me had me aroused and horny in a flash.

"Did you know Joseph?" I asked between rounds of practice.

He nodded. "I did. I knew his father, too."

"Both of them worked for the family?"

"Yes. Both died in the line of fire, too."

I sighed, feeling my face tug down with a deep frown. I hadn't even met Joseph, but I was aware of the day he was killed at that first place I stayed at with Romeo. The more I lived with Romeo and got to know more and more members of their organization, the harder it was to remind myself that they could all die. Sure, we were all getting closer to our deaths with every minute that passed, but these men were soldiers, fighters, spies, and protectors. They put themselves on the line for their leaders, much like the military did, and I couldn't help but worry about each and every one of them, regardless of how well I might know them.

It was a lot like Liam's situation. Or Mr. Bardot, Nina's deceased father. He was a military man like my old friend was, and I had utmost respect for their service. It was different, this privatized army of the Constella Mafia, but still similar.

"Did you get to know him much when he was on the security detail at that house?" Max asked.

I shook my head. "I was only there the one day and night. But I wouldn't mind going back there."

Max smiled. "It's a nice building. I believe it had been in the family for a long time, but vacant for many years."

"It needed work. It would be a big project to renovate."

"That was Romeo's plan. I think he wanted a project to preoccupy himself with while Dante had his new life with Nina."

I never once thought Romeo was struggling with Nina being in the Constella Family now. But I could see Romeo wanting his own space as a bachelor there. "And a project to preoccupy himself from the guilt about those three soldiers dying on his watch?" I guessed.

Max paused in reloading a gun. "You haven't been around for long, but you sure know that man well."

I smiled. "He told me a little about it. Survivor's guilt. Then again, I assume that this 'business' has a high death count."

"It does. And Romeo is aware of that. He's grown up with this life and knows how dangerous it is. I suspect those three soldiers hit him so hard because he was personally responsible for them. He was supervising that meeting with the Dominos. And Romeo is very protective of those closest to him."

I aimed through my sights but waited to actually practice.

"You seem to be helping him, though," Max said.

I raised my brows at him. "How?"

"By being another 'project' for him. Someone else to protect in a different way, in a way he's never been overprotective before."

I smiled. "Are you saying he's never had a girlfriend before?" *Yeah, right. That can't be true.*

"Are you saying that you think you're just a girlfriend for him?"

Whoa. That's blunt. My cheeks heated with a flush.

"What I'm saying is that you're giving him another purpose to live for. Not just for the family and for working for Dante. But for love. For a future."

"I've got to say, Max, you're the most perceptive soldier I've met yet."

He nodded. "You're welcome. I think."

"I do miss that house, though. Maybe it was because of the trauma being so fresh and not knowing where I'd go or what I'd do, but it clicked with me. I could see it being fixed up and modernized."

"That makes sense. At a time of turmoil, it was something to scrub clean and start over with."

"Well, yeah. But it's not my place to fix up."

"It could be. You and Romeo there while Dante and Nina start another family in the big house."

I watched him, wondering if it could be possible. "But if it's not secure, with those bikers creeping close and killing Joseph…"

He shook his head. "Nah. It's not impossible. I think Romeo moved you so quickly because he was nervous at the moment. With more preparation and installing cameras, that property could be as safe as any other in the Constella empire."

Huh. I enjoyed having *a* place to stay with Romeo, but the penthouse wasn't my style. I suspected it wasn't Romeo's, either. We'd hopped around a lot lately, and I wondered how Romeo would feel if I asked him about staying there when we could.

Assuming Max and Nina and Eva are right in saying I'm more than just a fling or girlfriend for him...

I planned to ask Romeo about the opportunity to renovate that house. It would give me a good thing to busy myself with.

After the shooting practice, Max saw me back to the mansion where Nina lived with Dante. We had arrangements to go to a store to set up her baby registry, and I was excited to do this with my best friend. Some days, I still couldn't believe she was pregnant. Romeo and I didn't use protection, but I wasn't in a rush to get pregnant. Not until I knew what I was to him.

Hah. As if I'd ever turn down sex with that man. I smiled as I thought about how rabid we were for each other.

On the drive to the mansion, my phone rang and I answered, assuming it would be Romeo.

"Hello?"

"Are you through with those bad men yet?"

I clenched my teeth at my mother's voice. "How did you get this number?"

"I asked Elliot to find it. He's got private investigators, you know. PIs who track down criminals like the man you were with."

"He's not a bad man." I was wasting my breath arguing with her, but it was instinct to defend him. He did bad things, but he was a good man. I knew that with every fiber of my being.

Even if he was morally gray, I couldn't imagine my life without him.

"Your father and I will disown you," she threatened.

"I thought you already had," I retorted.

"If you insist on running off with that bad man, you won't be any daughter of ours. We raised you better than this. We taught you to do the right thing and look forward to stability with an honorable man like Elliot. You—"

"Don't contact me again." I hung up, seething, and quickly set the phone to block that number.

Fucking Elliot. Of course that slimy lawyer found out a private number. He was more corrupt than any Constella.

Being stuck in a traffic jam didn't help my mood. After dealing with my mom, even for that short amount of time, I wanted to run. To move. I missed the energy of being at the shooting range. Sitting here without any means to vent, I exhaled a hard breath and glowered out the window.

She had no right. She had no place to call and badger me like that, and I wondered if she would ever stop.

My phone rang again, and I frowned at the unknown caller number.

"What?" I answered, half-expecting it to be my mother again, disguised by using another number.

"Wow. What kind of a greeting is that for an old friend?" Liam asked, laughing dryly.

"Liam!" I smiled, immediately happier to hear his voice. "I didn't recognize the number."

"Oh. Right. I had to get a new phone when I got Stateside."

"You're officially home? For a visit?"

He sighed. "No. I'm, uh, here for good."

I blinked, shocked. I always thought he'd be a military man for life. Static cut through the line, and I missed every other word of what he said next. "Huh? You're breaking up."

"I'm moving home," he said. "Wherever home will be."

I bet he could stay close to me and Nina!

"I'm hoping you can help me," he said, even though I had to guess at a couple of the words.

"Help you? Help you move?" *Like, physically?* I couldn't see how he'd have much to move after so long in the army. What possessions could he have accumulated in the service, always on the go and often out of touch?

This call was sort of out of the blue, but his request for help was even weirder. Liam was independent and stubborn to a fault, never wanting to ask *anyone* for help. He was a go-getter, and I knew for him to ask me for assistance, he really needed it.

"I'm in Utah," he said brokenly.

"What?"

Static cut through the call.

"Did you say Utah?"

"Yes, I—"

"Liam, the call's breaking up."

"I'll call again soon, okay?"

"Yeah. We'll catch up more." We would, and hopefully, not over a call with crappy reception. If he needed a place to stay, Romeo would let him stay. Because if it would make me happy to see my childhood friend, he would move heaven and earth to make it happen. I didn't think this with any degree of greed, only honesty.

This wouldn't have been a good time to catch up with Liam, anyway. We pulled up to the mansion, and Nina was ready to climb into the backseat with me.

"What took so long?"

"Traffic," the driver and I replied in unison.

"I just got a weird call from Liam," I told her.

"Really?" She smiled, excited. While she didn't know him as well as I did, she hadn't forgotten him. She was familiar with him via my friendship, and they'd gotten along fine when we were younger.

"Yeah. Just now."

"What was 'weird' about it?" she asked.

I filled her in on the few details that he'd shared when the call wasn't broken up. When I mentioned the preliminary idea that Liam could visit and stay somewhere nearby, Nina nodded. "Oh, sure. Dante said they have so many properties, they could live somewhere different every week and not repeat residences."

I raised my brows and blinked. "Wow." Sometimes, acknowledging the family's wealth meant imagining a staggeringly high amount of money.

Once we reached the store, we shifted from talking about Liam and any Constella properties to discussing baby things. We *ooh*ed and *aah*ed over all the adorable outfits, and we both admitted we had no clue what some of the apparatuses and tools were for. Most seemed to be involved with breastfeeding, and I reassured Nina that she had plenty of time to research and prepare.

"I can't believe he doesn't want to know what the baby's gender will be," I commented of Dante's refusal to find out beforehand.

Nina shrugged. "Well, he's already got a son. Maybe he wants a surprise this time."

To each their own, I guess.

When we left the shop hours later, *we* were the ones who got a surprise. An unpleasant one. Standing next to the car where the drivers would be waiting for us was a scowling man. He looked haggard and aged, like he'd failed to keep up with the plastic surgery necessary to appear youthful.

I didn't know who he was, but the pair of rough-looking men flanking him were familiar. I'd never met them, but they reminded me too much of the men who'd come to the cabin for it to be a coincidence.

They kept their attention on us as we stopped short in the small parking lot. With them standing between us and the car, we had no easy means of escape.

"You're a dead man walking, Giovanni," Nina said, glowering at the shorter, older man between the two guards.

Giovanni? This had to be Stefan, the leader of the other family. The two-timing, scummy Mafia boss that Romeo and Dante had identified as one half of their biggest problem.

At the sound of footsteps behind us, too close for comfort, I lowered my hand to my open purse, wanting the comfort of the handgun in there. A quick glance back showed that two more men had come up behind us, preventing us from running into the store.

The man in the suit smirked at my best friend. As he pulled up a gun and aimed it at us, I stepped forward and shoved her behind me. I'd be damned if she was targeted. Vulnerably pregnant and unarmed, she had to stay back.

"What the fuck do *you* want?" I demanded, hoping I sounded a lot braver than I felt.

27

ROMEO

Franco gave me a heads up that Elliot Hines was talking about meeting with me, and at first, I was skeptical. I assumed that he wanted to discuss Tessa, and if that was the case, I would not budge. I didn't care what he had arranged unofficially between his parents and hers. It wouldn't stand in my way of a future with her.

When more hints came to me through the spies that worked for us, I decided I'd cut to the chase and go to the asshole. If he couldn't man up to ask me to meet with him, he was either a coward who was afraid of the Constella name, or the rumors about his interest in speaking with me were nonsense.

I showed up, alone, and told his sex kitten of a secretary why I was there. "I'm here to speak with Hines."

She smiled, a practiced expression of patience that I doubted she felt. "I'm sorry, but Mr. Hines isn't available at the moment."

"Yes, he is."

She blinked, maintaining that air of patience but seeming curious. "And who might you be?"

"Romeo Constella." I stared her down as she looked at her computer monitor.

"Hmm. I don't see you in the books for any time this week. Are you certain you've made an appointment?"

I set my hand on her desk and leaned in, letting my jacket slide open until she saw my gun holster. "I don't make appointments."

She sobered, looking at my gun and keeping that polite smile plastered. "Oh. I see."

"Do you?"

She slowly smirked as she raised her brows, indicating for me to look at the cameras in the corner of the receptionist room. "Mr. Hines's security personnel can see too, you know."

"Who? The fucking bikers?" I mocked as I looked her in the eye.

"Mr. Hines isn't available, sir. If you would like—"

I walked past her, heading for the only door she safeguarded.

"Hey! Wait just a moment now. You can't—"

I could. And I did. I wrenched the door open and strode in, quick enough to close the wooden panel before she could follow me in.

"Who the fuck—Oh." Elliot Hines recovered from his shock. The scowl of annoyance fled his face as he smiled. "Constella." Then he rolled his chair back and tilted his head, indicating for the whore on her knees to scamper off. She wiped her face as she got up. Without sidestepping, I let her pass me on her way out.

Elliot zipped up, looking mighty pleased with himself for buying a blowjob.

"Am I interrupting?" I asked dryly.

"Not with anything I can't get whenever I want."

Cocky moron.

"I doubt you care if you *are* interrupting, anyway."

"Correct. I don't give a fuck about your agenda."

He smiled. "This is just a pleasant stop by, then?"

"No. I heard that you've been wanting to speak with me. I suppose you're too scared to come out and tell me directly what the fuck you want, but I've got a guess."

"Oh?" He cocked his head to the side, causing his thinning hair to shift over. It wasn't a combover, but it soon would need to be. "What's that guess?"

"Tessa West."

Elliot laughed and rolled his eyes. "I have heard that she was staying with you."

"Not just staying with me, motherfucker. She's mine." *Forever.*

He waved his hand flippantly. "Okay. I don't care who that fat ass ends up with."

Anger coursed through me. I resisted the temptation to pummel my fist into his face for that insult. Tessa wasn't fat. Not at all. Instead of letting his taunt get to me, which I knew was his intention, to rile me up, I waited for him to continue.

"Her parents always thought that I'd settle for her. That I'd lower my standards to marry her." He rolled his eyes again, looking like a pimpled, lanky, balding nerd. *His standards?* I bet that whore was paid double time to even look at his nasty, tiny dick.

"It would be an act of charity to even give her my attention for more than a quick fuck."

I smiled, slowly and sinisterly. Tessa would never let this creep near her. He'd never know the perfection of her body.

"She's not smart enough for someone of my position."

I snorted. "Your position."

He nodded. "My position as mediator for several influential members of society."

This kept getting better and better. "Let me guess. 'Influential' men like Stefan Giovanni and a dumbass named 'Reaper'?"

He furrowed his brow a bit, not liking how I made fun of his clients, but he caught himself quickly and wore one of those smarmy smiles again.

"That's why I considered arranging a meeting with you, Mr. Constella. To discuss an agreement with their corporations."

"Corporations?" I shook my head. "Cut the shit and call them what they are. A biker gang and a has-been Mafia Family."

His jaw slid as he clenched his teeth. "We are interested in speaking with representatives from your father's organization about—"

"No. Don't try that bullshit with me. I am his second in command. It's not my father's organization. It's *ours*. Anything you want to tell him, you tell me. I won't let a piece of shit like you waste his time."

"We would like to discuss the parameters of a potential agreement."

"Speed it up," I warned. I'd had enough with the filler.

"Mr. Giovanni is interested in a lease for a piece of property associated with your organization's portfolio. They would like to collaborate on a collective use of the land for distribution of their products."

We had so many properties I couldn't keep track of them all, but knowing this schmuck was talking about the gun routes the Devil's Brothers MC was interested in setting up, I had a decent idea of what areas they were likely looking at. Regardless of what lease or property they wanted, the answer would remain the same.

"Fuck no."

Elliot frowned. "What?"

"No. The Constella Family will not do business with any Giovanni or Devil's Brother."

He shifted in his seat. "I would like to add—"

"Add whatever the fuck you want. Our answer will remain a no." Taking one step closer to loom over him, I warned him further. "Do not bother us. Anyone who fucks with the Constella Family will lose. No one gets what they want from us. No one ever wins."

The bastard smiled, almost sniggering as he chuckled. "It sounds like *you* don't win either, Mr. Constella."

I arched a brow, humoring him with this illusion that I could be patient for him.

"I heard that you lost a few men recently. Three well-respected and prominent soldiers."

I breathed through my nose, counting down from five to temper my reaction and hide it altogether. Of all things for him to say. Of all places he wanted to take this conversation, that shouldn't have been it.

"I heard that you got them killed."

Fury built within me. He was trying to taunt me, like he had any fucking upper hand. But I kept my cool. Being with Tessa had helped me get over my guilt, and I knew deep down that I hadn't directly caused those men to die. I hadn't been at fault for Mario turning traitor on us in that incident and setting us up.

He knows a lot more than that. If this asshole could toss out details like that, he had insider information about much more. This lawyer wasn't just a player with the Giovannis and the Devil's Brothers. He was included in more than the basics to know about Mario leading three Constella soldiers into that trap.

I stared at the spineless bastard, knowing one thing had changed.

Killing Elliot hadn't been an option before. To do so would be a strike against the Giovannis and Devil's Brothers, and we had to strike well, not rashly.

Now, though, I understood that Elliot Hines wasn't just an associate. He was part of the planning process. He was a confidante.

And they all need to fucking die.

They would, starting with his piece of shit who dared to taunt me about my failures.

No more waiting. No more being cautious for all the ripples that might fan out as unwanted consequences from a murder or hit.

Elliot Hines's days were limited. As soon as I updated my father about this conversation, I would strike.

As I stared him down and let him panic with my silence, he seemed to grow more and more frustrated. Twisting his lips as though he struggled to keep his words in, he glowered and scowled.

"Stop fighting with my clients," he warned. "Don't interfere with their plans."

Their plans are fucked, dumbass.

Because they wouldn't live long enough to see them pan out. Not if I had anything to say about it.

After one last long look of malice, I turned and left without a word.

I'd kill this man soon enough, and I gloated on the triumph of knowing he'd live in fear until the moment I ended his life.

Good riddance, motherfucker.

I wouldn't have to worry about his being an obstacle in the way of making Tessa mine. And I wouldn't need to stress about his being a player in this war against the Giovannis and bikers, either.

He'd be dead before nightfall.

The thought made me smile, and I couldn't wait to share this news with Tessa.

Killing her rapists was one act of generosity.

Ending this fucker's life would simply be one more example of how much she mattered to me—another demonstration of how far I'd stoop to show her that I would go to the ends of the earth to secure her happiness.

28

TESSA

"What the fuck do you want?" I shouted at Stefan when he didn't answer me the first time.

The old man before us didn't match what I imagined he'd look like. Short and aging, he was a worn-out man. Not tall and strong, appearing like a formidable foe. Romeo, Dante, and Franco spent so much time talking about Stefan and Reaper as being their enemies and waiting for the opportune moment to hit back at them without risking the Constella forces.

This shriveled up man didn't *look* scary. His scowl seemed petty and pinched, like an expression worthy of a toddler throwing a tantrum. But the gun in his hand looked all too real.

I hesitated to bring my gun out of my purse, but in that moment as he sneered at me and Nina, I was so glad that Romeo was the over-the-top protector that he was. Right now, I was relieved that he insisted that I never leave the house without this gun on me.

The guards and driver had to be incapacitated to not be defending us, but that was another worry for later. Nina—and her baby—were priorities. I had to keep my friend safe and also make sure I could survive to see Romeo again.

Maybe his protectiveness was rubbing off on me.

"I want to end the Constellas," Stefan replied. His voice was gravelly and rough, raw from overuse and likely from a lifetime of smoking. "I will see the end to this vendetta against the Constellas if it's the last thing I do."

"Fuck you," I drawled. "You'll never end us."

One of the Giovanni soldiers behind him grunted. "Oh. You consider yourself one of them already?"

Stefan grinned, nodding. "You're nothing but a convenient piece of ass he picked up somewhere."

Nina's fingers curled around the back of my shirt.

"You're just another whore," the guard said. "You're not a Constella."

Their words were intended to cut me. To wound me and lower my guard. It didn't work. I *knew* that I had worth. I was all too aware of how much I mattered to Romeo.

"Just get the fuck outta the way so we can have her," Stefan snarled, leaning to the side to see Nina.

"I don't think so." I held my arm out, bent at the elbow, to barricade her behind me.

"You ain't anyone to tell us how it's gonna be."

I tipped my chin up higher, riding on this high of defending my best friend. "You're not getting near us. Not if you want to survive and finish out your pathetic lives."

My heart raced, and I licked my lips before I swallowed. With my mouth this dry and my breaths whipping in so fast as I fought the panic rising to the surface, I tried to look into the SUV and see if the drivers were dead or just unconscious. They'd never leave the scene if they could. They'd remain with us, watching from outside the shop.

"We want her," Stefan said. Then he shrugged one shoulder, laughing mirthlessly. "Ah, hell. You too. We'll take both of you even though she's the only Constella, breeding another motherfucker in her belly. If you're Romeo's whore of the week, we'll take you too."

"That's not going to work." I said it as a bluff, hoping he wouldn't call me on it.

"It will, you dumb bitch. It will. If I can't kill those fuckers, then I'll hit them where it'll hurt. I'll take their women, and they'll be so fucking mad they'll slip up and walk into any trap I set."

I shook my head, nervous when the guards crept up behind us, forcing us to walk forward.

Holding my arm out around Nina, I kept her close. Her back was to mine, and we paired up in facing them off.

Another SUV was parked behind the one we rode over here in. The backseat door was opened by one of the Giovanni guards, and he gestured for us to get in.

"Now, bitch. Let's go. Both of you," Stefan ordered.

"I don't think so."

Stefan aimed his gun lower, likely planning to hit me somewhere that wouldn't kill me quickly. Before he could have a chance to shoot, I brought my gun up and aimed at him.

"Run!" I shoved Nina to make a dash for it as I fired at Stefan and his men. I dropped as I fired, a trick I'd learned from the soldier who sparred with me and Max at the shooting range.

Gunfire filled the air, and with my chest squeezing tight with anxiety, I could barely drag in a breath to stay steady on my feet and keep my head clear.

Shouts rang out around the shots. Tires squealed on the pavement. Pedestrians and others near the store shouted and cried out in terror.

I stayed low to the ground, hoping no one would aim at me with the dusk setting shadows over us. Fear claimed me, but the rush of adrenaline kept me as focused as possible. I couldn't give up now. I had this. I could fight. I could shoot. And as soon as I got back on my feet, I would aim again and again.

Sheer luck had to be on my side because no wounds stung my skin or warranted a fall to the ground. I didn't know if I'd hit anyone, but I wanted to cling to the fortune that no one had hit me.

"Get her!"

I tensed as I scrambled back on my feet. Slamming my hand to the bumper of another car that I'd crawled to, I stood and searched through the smoky darkness and commotion for Nina.

They had to mean her. They said they wanted Nina, as an officially declared Constella as Dante's fiancée, pregnant with his child.

But they hadn't forgotten about me. A firm set of fingers wrapped around my wrist. Manacled by one of the Giovanni men, I lurched backward as he pulled me toward him.

"Take her and go!" Stefan yelled.

Car doors slammed shut. More tires burned rubber and squealed on the pavement. All through the chaotic sounds drowning out my thoughts, I punched and kicked at the man who tried to drag me away.

My fear evaporated. Instead, red-hot rage took over me. This guard's hold on me was eerily similar to how those three rapists had overtaken me in the alley. The muscle memory of being captured sliced through my panic.

And I lashed out, striking at the guards and refusing to be a victim of anything, ever again.

29

ROMEO

"Carlos said there's three more Giovannis," Franco said as he slammed to a stop in the parking lot.

The driver who'd brought Tessa and Nina to the store was shot, but he was alive to call us. I'd just met up with Franco to tell him about the meeting with Elliot when Carlos contacted us about Stefan trying to take Tessa and Nina.

Carlos was alive but unable to move his left arm to get out of the car. His neck was bleeding fast, he said. Yet he pressed the button to call on the dashboard. The Giovannis had left him and the other soldier, Yuri, as dead. Yuri was breathing, but unconscious in the passenger seat, according to Carlos.

Without either men able to help Tessa and Nina, it was an emergency.

Franco sped us over, and even though I knew my father would be furious that we didn't contact him immediately, there wasn't any time. This was a matter of life or death. I would *never* forgive myself if Tessa was wounded. And he would never forgive me if Nina was hurt.

I ran out into the fight, shooting at the Giovannis, so easy to make out with their suits in the darkness of the evening. Flashes of white were revealed when they ran, their suits flapping open and showing their button-downs.

Franco ran out with me, and behind us were more Constella soldiers alerted to the situation.

How the fuck Tess and Nina were out with only two men was ridiculous, but it was an error they'd need to address later.

"She's back there!" Nina crouched low near another car in the lot. She must have run to safety. In the split second that I looked at her, I spotted no blood, but Franco found her and covered her as he rushed her to the car we'd arrived in.

I turned in the direction of where she'd pointed, and when I locked my gaze on Tess, I wanted to roar. A deep, fierce need to burn the world down rushed through me. Anger and rage braided into a tighter stranglehold on my soul.

Seeing any man with his hand on my woman was enough to send me into a tailspin.

I'd caught her like this before.

I saw her in this position over a month ago.

A man trying to wrestle her away, grabbing her arm and hauling her toward him.

The mere suggestion of anyone trying to capture her was unfathomable.

I ran closer, letting the soldiers with me cover my back and make sure I wasn't hit.

All of these Giovannis would die. Every one of these fuckers would be killed by my hand or the crew who came with us.

No survivors would be allowed, but the man trying to drag Tess further away would be *mine*. His misery would come from my hands. His death would be the result of my wrath.

"Let her go."

It felt too similar to how I'd found her. That night when the three men violated her, that was the mantra that filled my mind. The order for them to release her. To step back and stay away from her body. To remain out of reach and let her be.

This Giovanni bastard didn't see me coming. He didn't hear my yell to release her.

Tessa fought back valiantly. Kicking, punching, and lashing out, she wasn't acting like a helpless victim. She didn't make it easy. If I had the clarity to think straight, I would've realized that my insistence that she go through self-defense lessons and practice sparring had prepared her for this moment. I'd helped her get stronger and have the confidence and courage to fight back, and if I could stop and be rational for even a second, I would've been so fucking proud.

But I wasn't rational. Not at all. A crimson tide of fury had descended on my conscience, and I was feral, ready to kill, impatient to torture and inflict the maximum amount of pain to make this asshole regret touching her at all.

"Let her go," I repeated, growling it as I rushed between them. My interference broke them apart. Tess flew back, staggering so she wouldn't fall. Her gun had fallen, no longer in her hand, and she scrambled over the pavement to pick it up and hold it at us. At him.

I barely took a moment to look at her. She was standing. She was breathing, panting furiously fast as she stared at me capturing the man in my arms.

Against me, he had a better, more level fight. We were the same size, but the difference between us lay in the raw fury that charged me to hit back harder and hold on to him tighter.

He wasn't going anywhere. Except to meet his fate in the slowest, most pain-filled means possible.

"Go," I ordered Tess. My voice was already hoarse, but I could swallow it down. Forcing my throat to work past the panic that clogged there, I tried again and again as I locked my gaze on her.

She's alive. She's free. She will be all right.

It didn't matter how quickly or how many times I forced that thought through my head. It wasn't easy to believe it.

She nodded, still gripping her gun with both hands. No marks showed on her skin from what I could see. If I spotted so much as a bruise, I would erupt from uncontrollable rage.

"Go." I jerked my head toward Franco's car. "Go home and wait for me."

I'd need hours—days and nights—of reacclimating to the knowledge that she was mine and she was unharmed. Seeing another man's hand on her had triggered such a darkness that I would need to dial down to be back to my normal capacity of sanity.

I wanted to hold her, to soothe her and caress her until all traces of distress faded from her being.

But I couldn't. Not yet. Only after I removed this man from the face of the earth could I go back to that degree of calm.

Franco rushed closer, helping Tess retreat to the car. He caught my gaze and nodded once. I didn't need to explain. He knew what I had to do. What I was impatient to do.

"Get him to the warehouse," I told the soldier nearest to us.

Handing the Giovanni to him was the only surrender I could allow. On the drive over to the warehouse where we took our enemies—one old brick building among many that served this morbid purpose—I thought ahead to the twisted glee and pleasure that would come from torturing this idiot who'd dared to try to capture Tess.

By the time I strode into the warehouse and found the man tied to the wall, I was prepared. I let the darkness stream through me, firing up my nerves. Soaking in the sweet anticipation of unleashing my anger and fury, I stalked closer and grabbed a knife from the table where different tools and blades waited.

I could take hours and hours, carving out pieces of him, but I doubted I had the stamina to last that long. This brutal wave of intense malice would burn out, and I would be left weaker and spent.

Until that moment, I doled out my fury on this soldier. Looking at him bleeding out and begging for mercy, I saw the rapists in him. My mind flashed back to the vision of his hand on Tessa's arm. Trapping her. Holding her against her will. Intending to drag her off and do something she didn't want.

I had yet to learn what happened in the parking lot. Carlos and the other soldier in the car would tell us more. Tess could too.

I didn't *want* to know what this fuck planned to do with my woman. The very notion of him trying to exert power over her and hurt her in any fashion was a crime enough.

"Just kill me," the Giovanni begged. "You sadistic freak. Just fucking kill me."

I stalked back away from him, not rising to the bait. Killing him too soon would cheapen this effect. Ending his life would be surrendering and giving in too easily.

"You deserve every second of pain."

The man groaned as I punched his bloody face.

"You earned each moment of agony."

He fell to his busted kneecap that I sliced at then hit with a hammer.

The man was a bloody pulp, but he was still alive. How he hadn't passed out yet was behind my understanding, but I didn't care one way or another.

He closed his eyes, dragging in labored breaths. Tears streaked down his cheeks, and I relished the triumph of reducing this man to a shred of who he once was.

He wasn't strong and powerful. He wasn't complete and fit to hurt Tessa ever again. He was losing valuable parts of his body that would render him a sack of flesh and bones—not a man.

And only with that knowledge did I feel ready to kill him.

A swift stab of my knife into his heart ended him. My soul felt lighter and his life ended, but inside my mind, a turmoil of anger lingered.

Without a look back, I trudged away from the macabre mess. The men stationed here would handle it. I couldn't look at any one of them, still locked in this wild energy that killing him had unleashed.

I'd tortured him. Killed him. And yet, I was on edge. That was how fierce my fury was, how hot my anger coursed through me.

"Let me drive," a man said outside the warehouse.

"No." Another shook his head at me. "Change first, Romeo."

These men were under my orders. They didn't tell me what to do. But this was a brotherhood, too. All I could do, numb under this pressure to inflict pain, was nod and follow along.

The second man guided me to the all-steel room where I stripped and cleaned the blood off me. After, still as numb and on autopilot with this madness gathering in me, I dressed and got into the car.

They didn't ask where to go. No one would be stupid enough to inquire how I was feeling and what I might need. My head wasn't on right. My soul felt freer for killing that man, but in my heart, I knew I needed to see Tess, to feel her goodness and know that she was pure and right. A shining beacon of positive energy. To be the Yin to my Yang and let me get back to a balance.

My phone rang and buzzed on the drive, but nothing could make me answer. A nonchalant glance at the screen showed texts and calls from my father. From Franco. Even from Nina. But the only one that I locked in on was the text from Tessa.

I'm here for you.

She would be. And I could bank on that. I could depend on that soothing message and count on her presence to calm me down.

I didn't rush inside the penthouse, but I allowed no detours or distractions as I rode the elevator straight to our floor.

Our floor. Into this place that we were trying to fit into as *our* house.

Tessa and I belonged together, as a unit. Partners. And I prayed that she would be willing to accept me at my darkest.

In our room, she waited for me. In nothing but a robe, her hair still damp from a shower, she lay on the bed. She might have been close to dozing off, but she jumped up as soon as I opened the door.

"Romeo." She stood, cautious about rushing toward me, and she was wise to stall.

I shook my head. "I'm not… I need…"

She sighed, opening her arms and dropping the robe in one motion.

"I need you," I said as I took in her luscious, bare body.

"Then take me. Have me. I'm yours, Romeo. Always."

Again, I shook my head and gritted my teeth. "I can't be gentle. I'm not right up here after that." I tapped my temple. "Not after seeing that man trying to pull you away."

She stepped closer and gripped my chin lightly, prompting me to look her in the eye. "Use me, Romeo. I'm yours to do with as you please.

Vent through me. Indulge yourself in me because I won't ever go anywhere."

I closed my eyes at her reassuring words.

"I will always be yours."

I gripped her neck and held her close to kiss her, letting the dams burst on my pent-up anger and need.

30

TESSA

Romeo smashed his lips to mine. Our teeth clashed. His tongue speared into my mouth with such a rough demand that I gasped and tried to keep up.

When I told him to use me, to use my body for the rage that still had him shaking, I thought I knew what I was asking for. For a hard fuck. A twisted turn in the sheets with his desire out of this world with the fear I assumed he felt at seeing that guard manhandling me.

It might have only been the rage, though, because I'd never seen him this feral and fierce.

But I wouldn't retreat.

I wouldn't take back my offer.

This man was my everything, and I was bound and determined to show him that I wasn't a fickle lover. That I wouldn't cringe and hide when the going got tough.

I accepted him for all he was. When he was considerate and generous. And also when he was rough and deliriously imbalanced on the thin lines of anger and desire.

I loved him, truly and wholly. Even if I wasn't an official Constella. Even if I was just a woman he was fucking for a while.

My heart would remain true to him, and I intended to prove it now.

"I need you," he said once he broke the kiss.

I wheezed and panted, catching my breath with the abrasive but addicting press of his mouth on mine.

I nodded the best I could with his hand on the back of my skull, his fingers twisted into my hair. "I'm all yours, Romeo." *However you want me.*

My heart cracked at the desperate look in his eyes. Like he was stuck in this horrid residue of violence and danger, this razored edge of right and wrong, both of them getting twisted into a complicated bind.

He clenched his teeth as he growled, then kissed me harder. When he parted again, both of us ragged for air again, he said, "Unzip me now."

I hissed as he thrust me toward the floor. With his hands in my hair, his fingers curved around my head, he had the leverage to move me. I dropped to my knees and removed his pants and boxers from his waist, bracing for his dick in my mouth.

Sucking him off was a pleasure, but I was under no illusion that this would be easy.

Without further warning, he shoved his long, hard cock past my lips. All the way in. The head hit the back of my throat, and my eyes watered instantly.

He didn't pull back. Instead, breathing hard as he stared down at me, he studied me with a carnal look of adoration.

Once I adjusted to the sudden intrusion, more of my senses kicked in to taunt me. The soft yet ridged surface of him. The salty hint of his pre-cum. Every bit of tension in his thighs as I held on to his legs.

Then, he moved, rearing back until he almost left my mouth, then slamming back in.

Used to his preference for hard and fast, I breathed through my nose and sucked him in, teasing him to give me all he had.

This wasn't a gentle love-making. This wasn't an explorative fuck. He needed to vent. To feel me. And I was proud to be here for it, to be the one he wanted and desired.

He thrust into me, hard and fast, and soon enough, I was moaning and furrowing my brow with the increasing need to come. Slick, sticky cream slid down my inner thighs, but I didn't dare lower my hands to touch myself.

I'd offered myself to him. This was *for* him, and I could wait. I would wait. Besides, with the ferocity of his thrusts, if I let go of his thighs, I'd fall.

I didn't have a reason to worry about that. Within the next moment, he pulled out and lifted me to toss me onto the bed. Being airborne dizzied me, but as I landed on the mattress and bounced, I rolled over to wait for what he wanted.

Or course, he wasn't done yet. Of course, he wouldn't come in my mouth and let it be over that quickly. He was still unhinged and starving for more of the intimate outlet I gave him.

"No." He pushed at my hip, urging me to go back to my stomach.

I rolled over, getting onto my hands and knees as he crawled onto my bed.

All my senses were hyper-acute. I felt everything—the absence of him in me, anywhere. I heard his ragged breaths, coming out just as rapidly as mine were. I smelled my arousal and his too, but also that sharp scent of soap from our showers.

But when he pulled me back against him until I knelt in front of him, I reveled in the sight of his tanned arm snaking over my stomach, his tatted flesh such a contrast to my paler, ink-free skin. The muscles bulged as he held me up flush to him, and I shivered at the force of power he exuded. Against his chest, I was splayed wide open.

He didn't keep me waiting. In one hard slam inside me, he penetrated my pussy. I groaned at the deep slide, but he kept going. Back and forth, he fucked me hard, harder than ever before. Like he was running from the demons in his mind, he pounded into me while locking his arm over my stomach.

"More, Romeo. Take me," I chanted. Thoughts were impossible. I hardly knew what the hell I said, but it still wasn't enough. His whole body, so hard and primed to fuck me all night long, was wired with too much darkness, too much anger.

"Fuck me harder, Romeo."

He growled at my invitation to really unleash on me, and he did.

By pulling out and rubbing his dick along my ass crack, he hinted at how he could take this up a notch.

Then by pushing his slick cockhead at my rear entrance, he suggested what else he could try.

Fears of what those three men did to me didn't surface. They lingered in the back of my mind. I figured they would always be there, repressed or locked away in compartments I didn't need to revisit.

As Romeo leaned over to piston his fingers into my pussy, though, all I could think of was him. All I could focus on was the urgency to welcome him into me so he could push us both to the ultimate pleasure.

"Yes," I said on a breathy exhale as he pushed his dick in higher.

We were close to the nightstand, giving him access to the toys in the drawer. When he reached over to open it up, he couldn't grasp the handle.

"Get it out." He pushed me until I leaned over, and while I was bent, he growled and fucked me harder. Not all the way. Every inch he slid in burned so deliciously, and I delayed opening the drawer.

It felt too good. Too raw. Too real, and I closed my eyes and hung my head low to savor the heat of what he did to me.

"You want it? You want me like this?" he demanded as I arched my back and thrust my ass higher in the air, presenting myself to him.

"I do. I want you."

He responded by smacking my ass. "Get the vibrator," he ordered as he gave me smaller, shallow thrusts into my ass.

He'd never seated himself there, and I figured he'd need to go a lot more with the distance between our thighs. I couldn't wait. Now, tonight, he would enter me fully there. I just knew it, or maybe it was a carnal, naughty hope.

Once I grabbed the long length he instructed me to fetch, he brought it to my entrance and teased the tip through my leaking juices. That friction was sweet torture, and I let him know it by pushing back against him, hoping he put it inside me once and for all.

I was impaled, stretched by his dick in my ass, but I wanted the vibe in me too.

Moaning loudly, I relished the abrasion of my nipples over the bed. The hot, callused touch of his hand on my ass cheek. And finally, the thickness of the toy as he rammed it slowly into my pussy.

"Oh, fuck." My response was punched out of me as the vibrator lodged deep inside me. With it in there, firing up my nerves and pushing me closer to climax, he slid into my ass, inch by inch. It felt like forever, an eternity of him stretching and filling both my holes, but all too soon, he ramped up the speed.

His thighs smacked against the back of mine. His hand grew wetter with my arousal dripping out along the vibe and over his fingers, so he smeared it on my legs as he pistoned the toy in and out of me.

When he pulled out the toy, he slammed his dick into my ass. Then on the retreat, he'd plunge the vibe right back in. See-sawed with the double hardness in me, I was a goner all too soon.

In a glorious moment of tears, shouted curses, and gritty moans, I came just before he did.

"Fuck," he roared, stilling his shaft inside me as he spurted his hot cum.

I tensed and cried out through the absolute euphoria of coming so hard. Dizzy and overwhelmed, I rode through the pleasure from the pain, the release from the tension, and all the sweet relief of coming apart as my pussy clenched and throbbed.

"Fuck, Tess. *Fuck.*" He slowly pulled out of me, and I moaned at the drag on my sensitive flesh. His cum leaked out my ass as he removed the vibe, but he didn't release *me*.

In his arms, I sagged and went limp, too spent and wrung out to move. Catching my breath felt like an impossible feat, but he held me up with him until we could stagger into the bathroom. He carried me, clumsy in his steps. Pressed against his chest, I smiled sleepily at the evidence of how hard he'd come too.

So blissed out and dazed from the force of coming like that, I was barely aware of being in the bathroom, much less that he was running a shower for us. While he turned the faucets on and steam quickly filled the room, I leaned against the wall and hoped I wouldn't slide to the floor.

"Come here," he said softly as he gathered me into his arms.

Into the water, we went, and I was relieved that he took over the act of washing us both. I'd just showered. He had to have too, with his hair wet. What we did might have felt "dirty", but as an act of love, it felt perfect as well.

"My sweet, sexy woman," he crooned once we were rinsed off. Huddled together, we sighed and enjoyed the pressure of the water raining down on us.

"I love you. So fucking much," he said.

I grinned, knowing he'd feel the rise of my cheek on his chest.

No man had ever said those words to me, directly, and I didn't want to receive them without looking him in the eye.

"What?" I asked as I peered up at him.

He blocked the water from hitting my face, but still, we both squinted. "I love you."

"And I love you, Romeo." I sealed it with a kiss that felt tender and serious at the same time.

When he stepped back slightly, he gave me that somber expression of intense focus. "And I'm going to marry you. As soon as I can."

My cheeks hurt with how widely I smiled. "You are?"

"Will you marry me?" he amended.

I had been wondering what label would apply to me, and now I'd know. My heart swelled with love, and I held in a squeal of excitement that this bad boy wanted me to be his wife. "I can't wait to marry you, Romeo."

He smiled slowly, lowering to kiss me once more.

31

ROMEO

Fucking Tessa like that took the edge of the madness brewing within me, but it was the slower, more delicate and tender lovemaking the next morning that seemed to really "cure" me. In her arms, relaxing in knowing she was fine and unharmed, I cherished all that she represented.

"I did shoot at him," she said nervously when she recounted what happened with Nina at the store.

I shook my head. "I don't think you hit any of them."

She exhaled a long breath of relief. "I can handle your being the killer. But I don't know if *I* want to join that club."

I kissed her brow and smiled. "Me neither. I want to protect you, Tess. I don't want you to ever be in the position to have to defend yourself like that or take a life."

"I would have if it meant keeping Nina and me safe, but…"

I smiled wider and brushed her hair back from her face. "But I'll handle the killing."

She frowned. "I do want to keep up with the training. Shooting practice and maybe even some martial arts. I feel more confident to know how to fight back, even if I know you will be my protector."

I nodded. "I agree. And you will continue it. I'm proud of you, Tess, for fighting back. It's sexy as fuck." I squeezed her bare ass to emphasize that point.

"Please," she groaned playfully. "I think I need a teeny break from another round."

Later, after we dressed and moved out of the bedroom, she asked if we could move to the house that I had wanted to renovate. I wasn't opposed to the idea at all, and I looked forward to her making her mark on the place and getting busy updating it.

"You've been thinking about this a lot, huh?"

She nodded over a late breakfast. "I have. For a while, I wasn't sure if I was a girlfriend or what. When Stefan goaded me about not really being a Constella, I resisted the thought that I didn't matter enough to you."

As soon as we catch him, he's paying for putting that doubt in her mind. "You do."

"I know." She smiled quickly. "But as I tried to figure out who I am to you, I daydreamed a bit about fixing up that place. Nina said the family has so many properties."

"We do."

She perked up. "Hey, that reminds me. I might need to ask a favor."

I huffed a laugh as I stood. "Don't call it a *favor*. You'll be my wife as soon as I can arrange. Spouses don't need to exchange favors."

"Okay. Then I need to ask you something." She shrugged. "My friend Liam could use a place to stay for a while, so I was wondering…"

"Sure." I recalled the fondness in her expression when she mentioned her old friend. I also recalled the jealousy I felt at the idea of another man in her life. An envy that no longer mattered. She said she'd marry me. She said she'd be mine, and I could put faith in that. Tess was mine, and no one else's.

Especially not Elliot Hines, whom I planned to pay a visit to later that day.

"You don't even know what I was going to ask!"

"Were you going to ask if he could stay in one of the houses we own?"

She nodded.

"Then sure." I kissed her brow, hating that I'd need to leave for a while to deal with Elliot.

My father and Franco rode along with me for that particular trip.

After the bullshit that Stefan pulled yesterday before going into hiding, it was a given that we would eliminate our enemies once and for all. It felt like a constant waiting game to figure out the best way to strike, but today, right now, we would hit back in such a way that would hinder the Giovannis and the Devil's Brothers.

Elliot was clearly a high player in their schemes, and whatever those two groups were plotting, it made perfect sense to take out the men who were a part of that bigger goal.

Stefan and Reaper would continue to cause issues for the Constella Family. They wouldn't stop. They wouldn't give up. The only end we could count on was killing them all, and sooner or later, that would happen.

I hadn't been bluffing. The Constellas always win. We always come out on top. Yesterday was another example of it. Carlos and the other guard would live. Nina wasn't wounded, just scared. And Tess hadn't been captured.

Now, as we rode to Elliot's office, we would ensure we remained one step ahead of our enemies by taking out the slimy lawyer.

"Congratulations," Franco said once I told them that I'd proposed to Tess.

"Did you use one of the family rings in the safe?" my father asked after telling me congratulations as well.

I shook my head. "I'm taking her to the jeweler's after this stop."

My father scowled, looking out the window. I doubted he wanted the memory of Nina in danger, but he wasn't going to freak out about it. He'd called Tess and personally thanked her for looking out for her friend.

He didn't get it. That was the loyal kind of woman she was. No thanks expected.

I also explained that we'd move back to the house that I'd first brought her to. Renovating would be a good project to share with her, but Franco shook his head. "Update the utilities first, so you can have the surveillance installed. Then move in there."

I'd already planned on overseeing those steps, but I didn't have to tell him that. He spoke up out of care.

"When will you plan the wedding?" my father asked several minutes later.

I shrugged. "Whenever she wants. Preferably sooner than later. Why?"

"Trying to figure out if I can pace myself here. Baby on the way. *My* wedding. Now yours." He looked at Franco at the same time I did.

"What?" he asked, shrugging.

"Are you going to be next?" my father asked.

Franco smirked. "No."

"Never?" I asked, teasing further.

"Not going near the idea of marriage ever again. No thanks."

Again? That sounded… specific. But it wasn't the time to ask him about his word choice. We arrived at the legal office, and I let my father lead the way.

I'd already gotten a taste of violence in killing the Giovanni guard who put his hands on Tess. I gave my father and Franco a chance to vent some of that dangerous energy. Killing Elliot seemed anticlimactic, just a single shot to the head. The two bikers positioned at the building for security were taken to a warehouse to be interrogated, then killed.

All in all, it was an efficient day of work. My father and Franco left me to return to Tess, and I smiled at her excitement the whole ride to the jeweler's. I arranged for a private viewing of the entire store, but I wondered if other customers being here would prompt her to be less indecisive.

"They're all too expensive!" she exclaimed after the first hour of browsing.

I leaned over one glass counter and cleared my throat for the jeweler to come closer. "No more."

He nodded, hiding a smile.

"No more what?" Tess asked.

"No more telling you the prices when you ask."

She pouted.

"Choose whatever you want." If she took all night here, so be it. But I was impatient to make love with her and see my ring on her finger.

"There's so many choices," she argued. "Can't you pick?"

I shook my head, amused and entertained.

"Seriously." She crossed her arms and gave me a playful smile. "You asked. You pick."

I sighed, playing along. I closed my eyes and spun, then turned to spin the other way twice more. Pointing my finger out, I aimed at whatever lay in my path.

"Nice choice," the jeweler said, holding out a bluish diamond ring.

"It was random," I deadpanned.

"Ooh." Tess's brows raised as she looked at the ring. "I can't believe that worked. But, Romeo... I think this is it."

I chuckled, walking closer as she admired the ring. "Tess, I don't care which ring you pick, just as long as it's mine."

She grinned, holding up the ring and presenting it to me. "This one." She dropped it, and the jeweler shrieked.

I lowered to the carpet and picked it up, and I realized her ploy. On my knee, I asked her again. "Will you marry me, Tessa?"

She held her hand out and laughed lightly. "It would be my pleasure, Romeo Constella."

I slid the ring onto her finger, and after I stood, I pulled her close for a deep kiss, a promise.

Because this woman would always be mine, to love, to keep, and to protect.

32

TESSA

"I think it'll be fine," Nina said as I bustled through the kitchen.

"I know it'll be fine, but I'm still nervous somehow."

She laughed as I nitpicked about food lying out for the small engagement party she wanted to throw for me and Romeo. While she was the host, she planned to be a lazy one. Her pregnancy was going smoothly, but her feet hurt too often to stand for long.

"Nervous about what, though?" she asked, watching me fret.

I'd never had a party thrown for me, so that was a little anxiety-inducing, but it was the arrival of one certain guest that threw me off.

"I haven't seen Liam in years," I reminded her. "About six."

She nodded and munched on a carrot stick from the veggie plate. "Okay. But it's Liam. A friend from the past."

"I know. But I can't tell how he'll react to my being engaged to Romeo."

She frowned. "Like he might not approve?"

I sighed. "I don't know. I'm being silly."

"Not silly. I'm curious about him coming here to stay, but not out of fear he won't like Dante or Romeo."

I pursed my lips and drummed my fingers. "Curious about what?" I was intrigued too, but I wanted to hear if she felt the same about what made me suspicious.

"Hmm." She shrugged. "He's being vague in his calls."

I pointed at her. "Yes!"

"He sounded glad to have a place to stay, but he put so much more emphasis on needing to find work."

I nodded. "Maybe it's because he decided not to enlist again?"

"Maybe. And that's surprising too. I don't know Liam as well as you, but I always figured he would be a lifer like my dad was, in the service for a whole career."

With my friend being only in his early thirties, that math didn't add up.

"Not to mention the way he keeps warning me that he has a 'surprise' for me to see," I reminded her.

"Hmm-mmm. But hey, maybe Dante or Romeo could offer him a job here."

"Offer who a job?" Eva asked as she walked through.

"A friend," I replied before she exited, not staying to chat.

Regardless of my excitement and nervousness to see Liam, I was counting down the minutes until he'd arrive. I hadn't seen him in years, and I was happy that he'd stay. In a small way, I wanted him to approve of Romeo because he *wasn't* another member of the Constella Family. I was surrounded by those who knew Romeo already, and I was excited to receive an independent opinion of the man I loved.

Nothing would steer me from loving him, but in a ridiculous little way, I wanted someone else to see and admire what I'd found.

Just before the engagement party would start, I worried that Liam had told me the wrong time or day of his arrival or that he wasn't coming.

"Is he normally punctual?" Romeo asked.

I deadpanned at him. "He's just been discharged from the military. Of course, he's punctual."

"Hate to say it, Tess, but..." Franco made a show of checking his watch.

Numerous guests had already arrived. They were mingling in the ballroom of the mansion, out of sight so I could welcome Liam in the more private living area of Dante and Nina's home. But sooner or later...

The back door opened, and we all turned toward the glass doors sliding open from the patio. A soldier led my tall friend inside, but the surprise he'd been hinting at...

"Oh, my God."

Nina and I said it in unison, gawking at the adorable little blonde in his arms. A toddler. She peered at us all, clutching Liam's shirt.

He looked the same, yet not. Rugged, dressed down in jeans and a T-shirt, sturdy boots on his feet, and a ruffled mess of his short hair. He'd aged and had been hardened with his time in the service, but...

"A *baby?*" I exclaimed.

"Surprise," he said in a gruff greeting.

Romeo leaned toward me and pressed his fingers up under my chin, prompting me to close my mouth. I was so stuck in shock, I couldn't believe my eyes.

"Since when..." Nina was no better than me, puzzling it out.

"Well." Dante strode forward. "Since they've forgotten how to say a simple hello, welcome to our home. I'm Dante Constella." He held out his hand, and Liam shook it clumsily, looking like he'd never learned how to hold a baby.

"Nice to meet ya," Liam replied, looking at Dante quickly.

"A *daughter*?" I asked him. "You have a daughter?"

"Yeah."

"But… *how*?" He'd been gone so long, and now, all of a sudden, he was carrying an adorable little girl who somehow resembled him.

He shrugged. "I got a letter that I had a kid, and…" He whooshed out a long breath. "And here I am."

Here he was—here *they* were, and I lowered my shoulders and winced at how out of his comfort zone my old friend seemed.

"Recently?" Nina asked.

He nodded, raking his hand through his hair as he looked us all over. "Yeah. Very recently. Olivia is a very recent discovery in my life."

So recent, it seemed, that he was still getting used to the idea of having a child. His hold was awkward, but firm.

The second Olivia pouted, then sniffled with pending tears, Liam's eyes went wide, like he was bracing for a combustion.

"Shit. Which cry is this? What's wrong?" he was concerned, but his tone was more for a peer, an adult he commanded in the field, not a toddler.

She wailed, and a soldier covered his ears off to the side of the room.

"Oh, darling," Danicia cooed, rushing from the kitchen where she'd been lingering, away from the guests. "Want a hand with her?"

Liam nodded quickly, hope in his eyes as he handed the toddler over. "I definitely need a hand with her."

Romeo chuckled as the family's doctor bounced and swayed with the toddler.

Liam grimaced, watching how Olivia settled quickly. When I looked at Romeo, seeing the amusement lighting his blue eyes, I knew he'd take pity on my friend too.

"What would you like to drink?" Romeo asked as he held my hand and brought me closer.

I shook my head, surprised so thoroughly that I had yet to even greet him. "Hi, Liam," I said as we hugged. I stepped back to my man. "This is Romeo, my fiancé."

They shook hands, and Romeo, quick to notice anyone's discomfort and singling out when someone needed saving, repeated his drink offer.

"Got any decent beer?" Liam asked, half joking and half sarcastic.

As a member of the kitchen staff nodded and went to fetch his drink, I smiled at Romeo. Having Liam here would be… an adjustment. Or maybe it was the unexpected way he'd arrived with a small plus-one. Regardless, I was excited.

"Danicia seems to have Olivia smiling and happy," I commented as Danicia and Nina cooed at the girl over toward the kitchen.

Liam grunted a laugh. "Better than I can."

"Rough going?" Romeo guessed.

Liam sighed and glanced around as though scoping his surroundings. I caught him frowning again when he spotted Eva at the other side of the room, who'd just walked in while talking to Franco.

"Yeah. Very rough," Liam admitted. "Sorry I'm underdressed for whatever you've got planned tonight."

I patted his arm, feeling sorry for how bewildered he looked. That was Liam, though, rolling with the punches and making the best of any situation he faced. "You're going to have to fill me in on a *lot* more details. But later. Right now, I'm excited for you to meet the family before we join the party."

Romeo draped his arm around my shoulders, and I grinned up at him. Notwithstanding the surprise Liam brought with him, I was so happy, so thrilled that I finally *had* a family, one I could be proud to call my own. One I'd treasure forever, especially my hero who I couldn't wait to marry.

Printed in Great Britain
by Amazon